# 1

Christine Findon was going upstairs after breakfast to get sheets from the linen cupboard to make up the bed in the spare room for her friend, Vivien Richmond, who was arriving that afternoon to spend the weekend with the Findons, when she met a perfectly strange man coming downstairs.

He was in his early twenties, of medium height, slender, dressed in a loose pale blue sweater and tight black jeans, and had what Christine thought of as well-tailored fair hair. By that she meant that while being longer than she personally liked it, it had been skillfully cut, fitting his well-shaped head with a certain style, and not hanging around his face like bunches of dead weeds.

As they passed, he smiled at her charmingly and said, "Good morning, Mrs. Findon. A bit brighter this morning than yesterday, isn't it?"

She answered that she supposed it was, although she had not noticed if it was or not, and went upstairs.

As she went, she wondered if she might be going mad. She could usually recognise the people whom she met in her own home, or at least account for their presence there. But recently a number of strange things had happened and several times she had caught herself wondering if perhaps there were something the matter with her. Basically, she supposed that most of what she was suffering from was

1

simply an overdose of the human race, for she was one of those people who need hours and hours of solitude, almost daily, to remain what she was accustomed to thinking of as normal. But this in itself, she knew, was a sign of being not very well-balanced, and the moods of desperation that had been afflicting her more and more often lately were beginning to worry her. She had never realised before just how very bad she was at coping with people.

Going to the linen cupboard on the first-floor landing, she took out sheets, pillowcases, and towels and took them to the spare bedroom. She was a tallish, very slim woman, of thirty-seven with an absent-minded sort of charm about her sharp-etched face, brown hair, light brown eyes, and an odd grace about her abrupt movements.

The spare room had an unaired smell and she opened the window. As she stood there, looking out, she wondered why the strange man on the stairs had said that the morning was brighter than yesterday's. There was no sunshine, the sky was evenly cloudy and there was a damp little wind blowing, tugging at the few brown leaves left clinging to the trees and fluttering the ones already down on the lawn.

The lawn was an unenterprising rectangle, surrounded by an arid-looking herbaceous border, and the whole garden was enclosed by a high brick wall. The wall was really the nicest thing about it. It was of the same softly rosy brick as the house and would have looked wonderful with, say, peaches growing against it. And a passion flower, perhaps. And there ought to have been lilacs somewhere.

The house was at one end of an eighteenth-century terrace on the outskirts of the small town of Helsington, and was a joy to the Findons, as, of course, the garden might have been too, if they had ever got further than having vague good intentions about it. But the trouble was that a garden takes so long to get started. They had lived in Helsington, though not all the time in this house, for twelve years, but had never felt that they were there to stay forever.

There was no special reason for this. Henry was happy in his job and they were not planning to move. It was simply that, belonging to the generation which had grown up during the war, they had been evacuated here and there and had

had parents who had come and gone as their duties in armies or navies had permitted, both of them had always found it extraordinarily difficult to imagine permanence.

Christine looked round the room and checked the fact that it was satisfactorily dust-free. The Findons' daily help, Mrs. Deeping, was uncommonly efficient, and Christine had asked her to clean the room well the day before. It was a cheerful room with pale sea-green walls and a sea-green bathroom opening out of it. There were built-in cupboards, and only a small Georgian table with a gilt-framed mirror on the wall above it, serving as dressing table, belonged to the same period as the house. Turning the mattress on the bed, Christine started to make it up.

She had reached the stage of tucking in the lower sheet when the worry about the young man whom she had seen on the stairs, which had been simmering at the back of her mind, came suddenly to the boil, and stopping what she was doing, she hurried out on to the landing and went down the stairs to Henry's study.

"Henry," she said, "I think perhaps we've got a burglar in the house."

Henry looked round from his desk. Because it was a Saturday he had not had to go out to Colnehill, the school where he was Senior English master. It was on the outskirts of Helsington and was one of those progressive places where they worry much more about building the children's characters than about teaching them anything, which, as Christine saw it, often worked out excellently for the clever ones, because they taught themselves what they wanted to know anyway, but could be a little hard on the dull ones. Nevertheless, she was strongly in favour of her husband continuing to be employed there, for the teachers had almost as much freedom as the children.

Henry was reading essays that morning. These actually might turn out to be anything from the opening stanzas of some projected epic poem to a half-page devoted rather stumblingly to something very uninteresting that had happened during the summer holidays. He never knew what was coming. It was an important part of why he enjoyed his job.

"Isn't it the wrong time of day for a burglar?" he said.

His voice was soft and resonant and hardly ever expressed shock or surprise. This was one of the reasons why he was successful with children. Children do not see themselves as shocking or surprising and do not want other people to do so. His eyes were grey and clear and misleadingly innocent. Misleading, because he was not really innocent at all. In his heart, he was prepared for the worst in everybody. His brown hair was turning pepper-and-salt, he was about six foot two, if he troubled to stand really straight, which he seldom did, and his age was forty.

"But burglars seem to be so unorthodox nowadays," Christine said. "They might easily arrive with the milk."

"Well, what makes you think we've got one?" he asked.

"I saw him," Christine said, "coming down the stairs. He's extremely good-looking and very good-mannered. He said good morning and remarked on the weather."

"But you don't know him."

"I've never seen him before."

Henry looked at his watch. "And it's nine-fifteen. And he was coming downstairs you say."

"Yes."

"And we've got nothing of value upstairs. So don't you think it's more likely he was coming down from Marsha's room than that he came here to burgle us?"

"Henry!" Christine exclaimed, scandalized at the suggestion.

Marsha was their *au pair* girl. She had been with them for a month, and having her in their home was one of the strange things that had happened to them recently. She was twenty-two and extraordinarily beautiful. She was also a gentle, obliging girl, who expected Christine to mother her, which was something that she was not very good at doing, and who often had an unnerving effect on men of various ages. But she had never given Christine the slightest reason to criticise either her morals or her manners, as entertaining an unknown man in her room overnight would have done.

Henry got up from his desk. "I suppose you want me to come and look round," he said.

"We'll do it together," said Christine. "And perhaps you should take the poker or something."

"Not much point in it," Henry decided, "since I'm not a hero. If he's a real burglar, I'll retreat in a hurry and summon the police."

"Of course, he's probably gone by now," she said. "He was probably just wandering about the house, seeing if he could find any loose cash."

"And if he was simply making for the front door when you saw him, he'll be far away by now. Well, where shall we begin? Sitting room, dining room, kitchen, broom cupboards, storeroom?"

"Let's start with the sitting room," Christine said.

The sitting room was by far the nicest room in the house, long and high, with two tall windows that overlooked the garden and a dignified fireplace which was the very best imitation Adam. The Findons had put most of their best furniture in the room. This had been collected slowly over a number of years, though some of it had been inherited six years ago from Henry's father, who had also left them the money with which they had plunged and bought the house. Since they had done so, one of their pastimes, over drinks together in the evenings, was working out how much richer they were constantly becoming by having invested their money in this way. Every time that they heard of a house in the terrace being sold, and how much more it had fetched than it had cost, they celebrated with delight their own increase in wealth. Naturally, they realised that this wealth was not of the slightest use to them as long as they remained in the house. But still it was a pleasant feeling to know that the money was there, waiting for them, if ever they moved away. And if they hung on for long enough, the sum might end up by being considerable, for Helsington, in a discreet and snobbish way, was developing.

But the sitting room, this morning, was empty. They went on to the dining room.

They found the stranger there, together with their nephew and niece, David and Frances Winter, who were nine and seven respectively. Breakfast had been cleared away, and they were all seated at the table, painting pictures.

The stranger got to his feet immediately and gave Christine another glimpse of his charming smile.

"We're having a wonderful time," he said.

David frowned, apparently irritated that their wonderful time was being interrupted.

"Sit down," he said to the unknown man. "You're standing in my light."

David and Frances were another of the strange things that had happened to the Findons that autumn. They were the children of Christine's brother Ian, and normally lived with him and their mother Ena, in Highgate, Ian being a reader in economics in London University. But in October he had left for a three-months' lecture tour of various American universities, and because of an impulsive offer of Christine's to look after the children for them, Ena had been able to go with him.

So it could be said that most of the things that had been happening to upset Christine lately were her own fault, for there had been no compulsion on her to issue that invitation. Henry, indeed, had advised against it, saying that she wasn't used to children, and would find them far more of a strain than she realised. But she was fond of Ian and Ena, and of the children too, and had been in a glow of pleasure at her own kindliness. Then Ian and Ena had insisted on paying for an *au pair* girl to help look after the children, and so Marsha Lindale had come to the house . . .

Henry advanced and took a look at the stranger's painting. He and the children were sharing a paint box of water colours and a mug of mud-coloured water.

"Don't ask me what it is," the young man said. "I was going to paint a ship, but David says I mustn't paint what I see, but only what I feel, and I'm not sure if I really feel anything much about ships."

What he felt, apparently, was expressed by a puddle of reds and greens and browns, with some vague yellow streaks straggling outwards from it to the edges of the paper.

"Oh, you're a friend of David's, are you?" Henry said.

"Oh yes, we're great friends, aren't we, David?"

"Mmm . . ." David was too busy with his own painting to bother to answer properly. He was a pale little boy, with a fierce, emotional face and a mop of dark brown hair. His painting was mainly in greens, and made Christine think of a cluster of ferns, and had a kind of airy delicacy, which was quite appealing.

"Then you're . . . er . . . ?" Henry went on.

"You mean you don't recognise me?" the young man exclaimed. "Good lord, that never occurred to me! I *am* sorry. I'm Lew."

"Mrs. Heacham's Lew," Frances said. She was a stolider, more rational child than her brother, less wrapped up in herself. She had noticed the blankness on Henry's face and had realised that some explanation might be helpful. She had the same colouring as David, dark-haired, dark-eyed, but her face was broad and calm and she was inclined at present to plumpness.

"Lew—Louis!" Henry exclaimed, and suddenly beamed with pleasure. "No, I didn't recognise you. What an extraordinary thing! You've changed incredibly."

"It's the contact lenses, mainly," Louis Heacham said. "I don't suppose you've ever seen me before without glasses."

Henry could have added, "And you've grown at least six inches in the last five years, and cleaned yourself up, and cut your hair and got rid of your pimples."

Mrs. Heacham was the Findons' housekeeper.

And it was acquiring Mrs. Heacham that was the most extraordinary thing of all that had happened to them that year, so extraordinary that Christine sometimes felt as if she must have strayed out of her own identity. When she thought of the fact that she, Christine Findon, a schoolmaster's wife, not only lived in a beautiful if not very convenient Georgian house, but actually had a staff consisting of a housekeeper, an *au pair* girl and a daily help, when she was used to doing nearly all her domestic work herself, she felt as if she must have stepped over the edge of reality into regions of sheer fantasy.

Mrs. Heacham had been housekeeper to Henry's father for ten years before his death, when she had gone to live with a married sister in Canada, returning only recently. She had always been devoted, efficient, immensely respected by the Findons. She had come to them when Henry's mother died. Mrs. Heacham at that time had been a widow of forty-five whose husband, a joiner, had recently been killed in an accident on a building site. Late in life and unexpectedly, the Heachams had had a child, Louis, and a condition of her going back to work for Henry's father had been that she could bring her son with her. He had then been seven years old and had grown up in the household. Yet he had always been in the background, kept there firmly by his mother's strong, possessive hand, a situation regretted by old Mr. Findon, for with his two sons, Henry and Simon, seldom at home, Henry already teaching and Simon at Oxford, the old man would have welcomed Louis's company, would have liked to be allowed to show an interest in him and to help him along to a career. But Mrs. Heacham had had her own clear ideas of what was proper, as Christine herself had been learning lately. Louis had never been allowed to intrude on the family. He had always been there, a shadowy little figure, growing up in the attics and basement of the house, but it had been possible to spend a week or two in it and never catch a glimpse of him. God knew what he had made of his strange, submerged life. Anyway, when he was seventeen, only a few months before the death of Henry's father, the boy had run away and never come back.

Until today . . .

Henry said, "Your mother's never said anything about you, Louis—"

"Lew," Frances interrupted. "He likes to be called Lew."

"Lew," Henry said obediently. "I didn't know you'd made peace."

"I'm not sure if peace is quite the word for it," Lew answered with a smile, "but I thought, poor old thing, why not let bygones be bygones? I'm getting along all right, after a fashion, so why not be friends?"

"When did you get here?" Christine asked.

"Last night, about ten," he said. "Do you mean she didn't tell you?"

"No," said Christine.

He laughed and said, "Isn't that just like her? She's got a passion for secrets. But it must mean I've trespassed on your hospitality without your knowing. I do apologise." He was very suave about it.

"Oh, I don't mind," Christine said, "except that I like to know, in a general way, how many people are sleeping under my roof."

"What are you doing these days, Louis—Lew?" Henry asked.

"Not anything much at the moment," Lew replied. "I'm not exactly a shining light at anything. I've been a good many things since you saw me last. Door-to-door salesman, taxi driver, jobbing gardener . . . But it's been an interesting life. One thing I've never been is bored."

"Well, I'm delighted to see you again," Henry said. "Now I must get back to my essays. You'll be staying on for a bit, I suppose."

Lew glanced uncertainly at Christine. "For tonight, anyway, if that's all right. I honestly didn't know, you know, that she hadn't told you."

"Yes, it's quite all right," Christine said. Yet she was not at all sure what she felt about Lew Heacham. There was something rather slickly ingratiating about him. He was pretending to be carelessly sure of himself, yet it seemed to her that he was watching warily to see that he did not put a foot wrong. But that might have been simply because he was extremely embarrassed at finding that he had not been invited to stay and was trying to carry it off a little too airily. The children, at any rate, seemed to have taken to him, which was useful. They were inclined to be hypercritical and to show their likes and dislikes without any of the disguises that make life tolerable.

Henry went back to his study and Christine to the kitchen. She found Mrs. Heacham sitting at the table, drinking coffee. Christine did not know how many pints of instant coffee Mrs. Heacham got through in a day, but any time that Christine went to the kitchen there was a good chance that she would find the housekeeper with a cup within reach. She gave Christine one of her dark looks and said sombrely, "So you've seen him."

She was a small woman, who once, as Christine knew

from photographs, had been extremely pretty. She had had
curly fair hair, delicate features and a slender body which
she had held very upright, moving with a vigorous, springy
alertness. But age had shrivelled her. It had not filled her
out and rounded her in any way, but only tightened her up
everywhere. She was still as slim as she had ever been, and
as upright, but with a look of brittle fragility about her, as
if there were little left of her but bone. Her hair was grey
and she wore it, cut very short, with a contemptuous indifference to the fact that it was still fine and soft and could
have framed her face with charm. It was a small face, pallid
and finely webbed with wrinkles, and dominated by the
great grey eyes, the critical gaze of which Christine often
found immensely disturbing. Mrs. Heacham was wearing
a neat blue nylon overall, as she usually did in the mornings.
In the afternoons she would change into a discreet woollen
dress, over which she sometimes chose to wear a pretty,
frilly little apron.

"Yes, I've seen him," Christine said. "Why didn't you
tell us he was here? Henry would have been so glad to see
him again after all this time."

"It was late when he got here," Mrs. Heacham said. "I
didn't want to disturb you. But I didn't think you'd mind
if I put him in the attic. If the children hadn't found him,
he'd have come and gone without you being bothered."

"But we *aren't* bothered, don't you understand?" Christine said. "We're delighted. We're delighted for you. It
must be wonderful for you to see him again."

"Wonderful?" Mrs. Heacham said, as if the word puzzled
her. "When he's only come because he wants money? Is
there anything so wonderful about that?"

"Oh, I'm sure that isn't his only reason." But Christine
was not at all sure. It seemed a fairly likely explanation of
Lew's reappearance.

Mrs. Heacham gave a tight-lipped smile. "Why pretend?"
she said. "I've never been much of a one for pretending.
That boy's no good. He got his looks from me, the kind
of looks I had when I was young, but he got his character
from his father. He was no good either. It was a mercy,
really, when he got killed, because he was heading for

trouble, helping himself to money that didn't belong to him, and if I'd had to face the shame of him going to prison, I don't know what I'd have done. I've had to face a lot of things in my life, but that's something I've been spared. Till now. But I'll tell you one thing, Mrs. Henry, if that boy gets into trouble, I'm not going to lift a finger to help him. What has he ever done for me? I did everything, I worked my fingers to the bone for him, but did I even get thanks? No, he ran away and left me. And do you know, when he came here yesterday, it wasn't me he was coming to see? I don't believe he even knew I was working here for you. And did he say he was glad to see me? Did he say there was anything wonderful about it? No, I thought for a moment he was going to turn tail and run off down the street."

"But why did he come, then?" Christine asked.

"To see what he could get out of you and Mr. Henry," Mrs. Heacham said. "To play on your feelings. And don't say I didn't warn you. It's up to you now. As I said, I did my best to see he didn't bother you. But what happens now is up to you."

"All right," Christine said. "I'll remember."

She left the kitchen and went upstairs again.

She met Marsha Lindale coming down. As usual, when she saw the girl, Christine felt a slight shock, the kind of shock that anyone feels on coming face to face with beauty. Not simply youth and charm, which so often can be made to pass for beauty. Christine had a way of forgetting about these things when she saw Marsha, for she would certainly be quite as lovely in twenty years' time as she was now. In fact, when the lines of her face had strengthened and there was experience behind her innocent blue eyes, her attractiveness would be formidable.

She was small, slender, and supple, but with a suggestion of toughness about her, which Christine had discovered was in her character too, as the children had also discovered it. Though she was cheerful, gentle, and eager to please, there was a point beyond which she could not be pushed, even by those two masterful people. When Christine would have automatically given in to them, Marsha quietly said no.

They admired her immensely. She had heavy fair hair, with just a tinge of true gold in it, and skin as soft as flower petals. She was taking a course in Domestic Science at the college in Helsington, and of course had to have time off to attend her classes and to study, but still she managed to have plenty of time for the children.

Occasionally she liked to have long, serious talks with Christine and Henry about the state of the world, which worried her a good deal, and from time to time she obviously needed to make impulsive displays of affection. Her father had died years ago and her mother had recently married again and gone to live in South Africa, where Marsha's principles concerning apartheid did not allow her to follow her. So she really felt very much alone and in need of a home, and finding herself in the Findons' had been as lucky for her as it had been for them. At least it was giving her time to think.

As she and Christine met on the stairs, Marsha threw her arms round Christine's neck and breathed in her ear, "Darling, I love you!"

"That's nice," Christine said, and added, "I like your sweater."

Marsha had just finished knitting it herself. It was black, with an unbelievably intricate white pattern worked into it. She was also wearing black jeans and snub-nosed scarlet shoes.

"Do you? Do you really?" Marsha asked. "Would you like one like it? Not exactly the same, of course—different colours, navy blue and emerald green, perhaps, to go with that tweed skirt of yours—would you like it? I'd love to make one for you. If you'd like it, I'll go in to the shops this morning and buy the wool. I'll take David and Frances, shall I? It'll give them a walk."

"If you can pry them loose from their new friend," Christine said. "Have you met him? Mrs. Heacham's son, Louis—I mean, Lew."

Marsha gave an incredulous giggle and said, "Mrs. *Heacham's* got a son? Doesn't that seem utterly improbable? Why haven't I heard of him before?"

"You haven't?"

"Never."

"Then I suppose it's just that we'd all forgotten about him," Christine said. "He ran away from home about six years ago. He seems to have thrived on it, to judge by appearances. He used to be spotty and spectacled and terribly shy. That's all quite changed. But if you look into the dining room, you'll see for yourself."

"I can't wait!" Marsha cried and went racing down the stairs, while Christine went on to the spare room and resumed making the bed.

The sheets and pillowcases were of deep turquoise, which toned very nicely with the sea-green of the walls, and had sprays of white embroidery on them. They were a recent present from Ena, a part of her thank-offering to Christine for taking care of David and Frances. Ena had a wonderfully lavish way of spreading gifts around her, usually hitting on just the kind of luxuries which her friends had inhibitions about buying for themselves. Christine had not yet used these sheets. They had always seemed too special, somehow, even to take out of their cellophane wrapping. But a visit from Vivien Richmond qualified as a special occasion, and Christine was handling the sheets with pleasure, enjoying the texture of them, smoothing them out and tucking them in, when Mrs. Deeping came into the room, bringing her a cup of coffee.

Linda Deeping was a police constable's wife, and had been coming to clean the house three times a week for the last two years. Sometimes she brought her four-year-old daughter with her, if her husband's shift took him out during her working hours. This morning her hair was pink and she was dressed in a thigh-length pink dress and white lace tights. Christine never knew, from week to week, what colour Linda's hair would be next. Last week it had been a rather becoming shade of silver. The pink was not as successful. Her hair, her clothes, her husband, and her child all seemed to hold about equal positions in her mind as objects of interest. But she was a good-natured and very efficient young woman, who could come out of a room after moving every piece of furniture in it and cleaning every inch of it with not a wrinkle in her spotless dress or a hair out of place. Recently Christine had caught herself remembering the days before the invasion of her home by Mrs. Heacham and Marsha, when she had had only Linda's help, as a time of peace and calm and contentment.

"My Joe had his jaw bashed last night," Linda remarked placidly, as she handed Christine the cup of coffee. She went on: "You needn't have made the bed, I'd have done it for you."

"I'm not used to having so much help," Christine said. "I get the feeling I must do something for myself. How did Joe get his jaw bashed?"

"There was a man at a party down our way got drunk," Linda said, "and started beating up his wife. The others couldn't control him. Three of them there were, so you'd think they could have managed, but instead they go and phone the police. So Joe got sent along and tried to get the man to go on home quietly, so he needn't charge him, and the man took a swing at him and got his jaw. It's made his face look all crooked this morning."

"Didn't Joe take a swing back at him?" Christine asked.

Linda looked shocked. "That would've got him into real trouble. Not that he didn't want to. He often wants to, but you've got to learn not to do that sort of thing if you're in the police. I don't think people realise."

"How are Mr. and Mrs. Ditteridge?" Christine inquired.

Superintendent Ditteridge and his wife were the Deepings' nearest neighbours, and Linda Deeping's conversation often consisted of a running commentary on their lives. As a mere constable's wife, she regarded them with a good deal of awe, though this was tempered by having had the chance to observe the Superintendent's behaviour towards his dog, Pippy, a small cairn bitch whose nature was very demanding and, for her size, ridiculously ferocious. Pippy hated to be left alone and if she were, would wail till the nerves of everyone within hearing distance were in tatters. She also hated all strangers and would bite them in the ankles if she had the chance. So if Mr. and Mrs. Ditteridge wanted to go out together, the Deepings often had to dog-sit, which the Ditteridges sometimes repaid by baby-sitting for the Deepings' Maureen.

"Maureen loves it when they do," Linda had once told Christine. "They spoil her so and let her do anything she likes. It's because they've no children of their own, you see. That's why Mr. Ditteridge is like he is with Pippy. I wish you could see it, a stiff sort of man like him, who never forgets he's a Superintendent, the way he croons over her and says doesn't she want to come to Daddy. If some of those tough young constables could see him, they'd split their sides."

Joe Deeping, although one of the young constables, had never struck Christine as specially tough. He was a very silent young man, who, whenever possible, let his wife do his talking for him. In his spare time she sometimes made him do odd jobs for the Findons. From time to time he put in an afternoon in their garden, and sometime soon he was supposed to be coming to distemper the storeroom. This was a big room next to the kitchen, and had once, probably, been the kitchen itself, while the present one, a smaller, cosier room, had perhaps been the morning room. The store-room was a wonderful place for dumping all the junk in the house, trunks, buckets and brooms, a rack of tools, a step-ladder, odd pieces of furniture that the Findons had grown tired of but could not make up their minds to throw away, and cardboard boxes that might come in useful sometime. It was a dusty, cobwebby place, because the major under-taking of giving it a good turning out always seemed to be something that could be put off while something more urgent was done. David and Frances loved the room as it was. Dust and cobwebs seemed only to enhance its glamour for them. Their imaginations could change it in an instant from a magician's cavern into a wild West saloon or an abode of Martians, and they knew, of course, that they could make as much mess as they liked there without being criticised. However, they had taken a fancy to Joe Deeping, and were looking forward to the day when he would start painting, intending to help him with it while he entertained them, they hoped, with tales of blood and crime.

Linda and Christine finished Vivien's bed together, then Christine went downstairs and again interrupted Henry.

"I'm sorry to bother you, Henry," she said, "but I'm

still worrying. I'm worrying about having Lew staying here."

Henry turned round in his swivel chair and looked at her patiently. She came into the room, shut the door and sat down by the gas fire.

"I've been talking to Mrs. Heacham and she says he didn't come here to see her. She said, in fact, that he didn't even know she was here, and that when he saw her he looked as if he was going to do a bolt. So it looks as if he came here to see us, and if he did, turning up at an odd time like ten in the evening, it can only be because he needs help of some sort. Yet he hasn't said anything about it to us."

"Perhaps his mother scared him off doing it," Henry suggested.

"She said he came because he wanted money."

"I shouldn't be surprised if she's right."

"And she warned me against having anything to do with him."

"She's always been like that," Henry said. "She's always warned people against other people. She doesn't much like them to like each other. The best thing always is to take no notice."

"But what do you think Lew's been doing all these years?"

"Why not the things he told us?"

"Just odd jobs?"

"That sounds to me quite likely."

"Well, why didn't he get in touch with us sooner?" Christine asked. "It's his mother he's really been avoiding all this time, isn't it? And he must have known where we were, or he couldn't have found us when he wanted to. Don't you think it may mean he's in some sort of trouble now?"

"I shouldn't be surprised."

"You take it very calmly."

He put the tips of his fingers together. "What point is there in taking it any other way?"

"But suppose, for instance, it's trouble with the police."

"You've got the feeling he's a criminal type, have you?"

"Oh, I don't know," Christine answered. "And I don't

suppose I'd worry if we were here on our own. But we've got the children and Marsha. It's a lot of responsibility."

"I thought myself he'd turned out rather pleasant-looking," Henry said. "Far better than I'd ever have expected."

"Oh, he's very good-looking. I just thought there was something about him that didn't ring true."

"Come to think of it, there always was," Henry said. "It was very strange, you know, his childhood in our house. He spent most of his time in a sort of no man's land, playing fantasy games by himself, and soon turned into a fabulous little liar. Not a malicious or trouble-making liar, but just the kind that likes to build himself up as something much bigger than he is. And of course he was bound to break out somehow sooner or later. Running away and disappearing was one of the less troublesome sort of things he might have done."

"But what do you think we ought to do about him now?"

"Wait and see what he does himself."

"If only it weren't just this weekend, with Vivien coming . . ."

Henry sighed. "Yes, it's a pity about that. But you don't want me to ask him to leave, do you?"

"Oh no. I think I just wanted to sit and complain about things in general for a little while. They seem to be piling up. The Maskells for drinks, and perhaps they won't hit it off with Vivien and she'll show it, and then her being the speaker at the dinner tonight, where perhaps she won't bother to put on a good show, if she doesn't think the audience is up to her standard, and having her mock them all afterwards for being deadly provincials . . . Henry, I can't think what ever made me suggest her as the speaker for our poor little society. I didn't have to. All I had to do was sit silent and let someone else on the committee come up with a suggestion. But I always look forward to seeing Vivien until the time for it actually arrives, and then I start remembering what a strain it was last time and wondering what ever made me ask her. And now with Lew here, and Mrs. Heacham sitting out in the kitchen, looking like a sort of Medea, who's thinking out how to set about murdering her child, I really can't believe we're going to enjoy the weekend much, can you? But I wouldn't dream of turning Lew out. After all, he's a kind of a member of the family, isn't he?"

"Good, I'm glad that's how you feel," Henry said. "Now I ought to get on again with this work."

He swivelled back to the pile of essays on his desk, and Christine got up and left him to them.

# 2

As she came out into the hall, she saw Marsha, with Lew and the two children, just leaving the house by the front door. Christine supposed that they were going on a shopping expedition to Cleeve and Coleford, Helsington's biggest shop, to buy the wool for the sweater that Marsha had thought that she would like to knit for Christine. So it looked as if Marsha and Lew had very quickly taken to each other, and Christine wondered what Mrs. Heacham would make of that. She could be guaranteed not to like it and to show that she did not, and that was not going to help over the few days of Vivien's visit.

She was arriving on the 3:15 that afternoon. She had been invited to speak at the Annual Dinner of the Helsington Costume Society and the subject on which she had chosen to address them was Georgian shoes. She was an expert on costume, and had written several books on fashion through the ages, but footwear was her speciality. She was in charge of the footwear department at the Blanchland Museum of Costume in London, and would be bringing a collection of shoes with her. Christine knew that if Vivien put her heart into her talk, she could make a very good job of it. She was witty, had the art of appearing spontaneous even when she had rehearsed every word that she meant to say most carefully, could suggest that her audience of course knew

19

as much about the subject as she did and that it had been simply delightful of them to invite her to talk to them, and could win all hearts. But if she was not in the mood, she would show that she had not bothered to give her talk any thought because she had not really considered her audience worth it, would let everyone see that she thought the dinner itself inferior and that she could not wait to get away.

The society was actually a surprisingly active one for a town like Helsington. But then Helsington had a very nice little museum of costume itself, and though of course this did not compare with the Blanchland, it was a quite interesting collection. Its curator, Arthur Winslow, was immensely well-informed. So if Vivien decided to be haughty and condescending, it would be decidedly embarrassing for everyone.

She and Christine had known each other since they were students. While Christine had been taking a degree in English Literature, Viven had been taking one in Fine Arts. She had married for the first time while she was still at the university, but had gone on and finished the degree, then almost immediately afterwards had divorced her husband and taken a job at the Blanchland, where she had remained ever since. If she lacked stability in her emotional life, she was fidelity itself to her professional one. Her second marriage had lasted a little longer than the first. Her husband had been with the B.B.C., and for a time Vivien had enjoyed meeting the kind of people with which this had brought her in contact. But then she had met Barry Richmond, and very soon afterwards had persuaded her husband to let her divorce him. She had been married to Barry now for two years. Christine had never seen what was so special about him, but it looked as if Vivien had at last found what she wanted. He happened to be curator of the Blanchland Museum, so for the first time she was living with a man who shared her interests, and they were able to talk shop endlessly. He was a small, quiet man who hardly ever looked at the person to whom he was talking because he had his gaze glued all the time to Vivien, as if he could not see enough of her.

Christine set out to meet her at the station at about a quarter to three.

Going to get the car, she heard sounds coming from the garage, a soft whistling and a swishing of water. Entering, she found Lew Heacham cleaning the car.

He gave his wonderful smile.

"I thought, while I was here, I might as well earn my keep," he said.

"It's very good of you," Christine said. "Henry thinks there's no point in cleaning cars. But unluckily I need it now."

"Can you give me two or three minutes?" Lew asked. "I'll be done then."

Since it was half an hour before Vivien's train was due, and since it usually took under ten minutes to drive to the station, unless one were very unlucky with the traffic, Christine said that it would be all right, and she stood waiting while Lew went ahead with the job.

"A nice car," he said. It was an Austin Eleven Hundred, about three years old and had seen better days. "I don't suppose you've any use for a chauffeur."

"As you so rightly say," Christine replied, "we haven't."

"I've been a chauffeur," he said, "and I was a very good one. I looked splendid in uniform, and I know quite a lot about cars. I like them too. I'd never let a car go out in the sort of state this was in."

"I'm sorry," Christine said. "I know we rather neglect it."

She was recalling how he had looked six years ago, a pallid, rather sullen, seedy-looking young boy, with spectacles that generally seemed to have been mended somewhere with sticking plaster, hair to his shoulders and shirts and trousers of strange colours and depressing dirtiness. But now, even after cleaning the car, he looked neat and fresh, with just a slightly brighter glow in his cheeks than before, and with his well-tended hair faintly, attractively ruffled. She supposed that he had outgrown his need to rebel against his mother's standards and so had allowed his own actual desire to be clean and charming develop. Or had she got it the wrong way round? Were the well-built body, clear skin, and open friendliness the disguise, assumed because he had found that it made his way in life easier, and was there still someone shrinking, isolated, and resentfully bewildered inside? When you looked at his face carefully, there was something unformed about it, not really as clearcut as it seemed at a first glance. Not an easy face to make up your mind about.

She went on, "Your mother told me you came here partly because you wanted to see Henry and me."

"Yes, of course," he answered. "I always felt bad about the way I treated the family. I needn't have done it. I could've written. I could've said I was grateful for all they'd done for me. But at the time, you know, I just hated the lot of them, along with my mother. But one grows up and one begins to see what a fool one's been. So I thought, as I was in the neighbourhood, I could look in and make peace. If you wanted to, that is. And of course, I wanted to see my mother."

"Do you know she doesn't believe you even knew she was here?" Christine said:

He laughed. "That's just the way she talks. She won't let herself believe I came here to see her. She has to have her grievance."

That was true, but all the same, Christine asked, "How did you know she was here?"

"I wrote to her, you see," he said. "At her sister's, in Toronto. I'd got into this state of wanting to make peace. I'd found myself thinking, 'She's old, and one day she's going to die—it could happen any time—and how would I feel then if I hadn't even written?' So I wrote, just hoping she was well, and saying I'd got a good job, and that sort of thing. And my aunt wrote back to me to say they'd quarrelled and Mum was back in England, working for you. So that jolted me rather, because I hadn't really thought of seeing her again just then. But then I thought, 'What the hell, I'm not afraid of her any more, so why not come along?' That's all."

"And there was no special reason why you wanted to see Henry and me?"

His eyes suddenly focussed acutely on Christine's. "It *is* special in a way, finding out if you'd be glad to see me or kick me out. But if you're asking if I came to get anything out of you—help, money, anything like that—then no, I didn't."

"I'm sorry, I shouldn't have put it like that," she said. "It's just that your mother's so certain you're in trouble of some sort. And if you are—well, you know Henry. He'd do his best to help you."

"Yes, I know. And thanks. If I did need help, Henry's the first person I'd think of going after. Not Simon. He'd have half a dozen nice ways of saying he couldn't do a thing for me. That's what comes of getting rich. He really is rich, isn't he? He's done really well for himself."

"Yes, he's been very successful," Christine agreed.

"It must be a nice feeling." Lew gave the boot of the car a friendly slap. "Well, here's your baby, all prettied up for you. Talking of prettiness, though it isn't the right word, that Marsha of yours is something quite special, isn't she? How ever did you find her?"

"My sister-in-law found her for us to help with the children. I think she discovered her through the friend of a friend, that sort of thing. Of course we didn't take her on for the sake of her looks, but I admit they're a sort of bonus thrown in. It's her nature that makes her such a treasure."

"Is she going to this dinner affair of yours this evening?"

"No, she'd find it pretty boring. Everyone there will be about twice her age."

"It's just that it might affect my own plans for the evening. But if there are any other odd jobs you'd like me to do while I'm around, just tell me—if you really don't mind me staying on for a little while, that is."

Christine noticed that the time that he was intending to stay seemed to have extended itself since he had spoken of it last.

"Well, thank you for cleaning the car," she said, getting into it.

"A pleasure. I get restless if I don't keep busy. And if I just sit around Mum will have a chance to start telling me the worst about myself and we'll only quarrel and I'll have to disappear again. Would you like me to do some digging in the garden? Or I could sweep up the leaves on the lawn and make a bonfire."

"Oh, that would be wonderful," Christine said. "Yes, if you're looking for something to do, sweeping up the leaves would be perfect."

She raised her hand in answer to the little wave that he gave her as she drove off, and started off for the station.

In spite of the delay, she had ten minutes to wait until Vivien's train was due. She spent the time walking up and down the almost empty platform. The station was a bleak, windswept place on the edge of the town. Arriving there by train, it always felt as if one were arriving nowhere in particular, as if the train must have stopped there just for some whim of its own. She had a scarf over her head and kept her coat collar turned up and walked fast, because the wind had a bite here that it had not had in the more sheltered part of the town. But she felt braced by it, not only because of the fresh air, but because it was the first part of that day that she had had to herself. During the last few months she had taken to snatching all the moments of silence and solitude that she could.

She saw Vivien as soon as she stepped out of the train. A man in her compartment helped her out with her luggage and Christine saw her thanking him with the peculiar sweetness and warmth that she could switch on like electric lights when she happened to want to. She had two large suitcases, which struck Christine as a lot of luggage for a weekend, until she remembered that one of the cases would contain the collection of Georgian shoes from the Blanchland that Vivien was bringing to exhibit at the dinner. She saw Christine, waved a greeting, and as they met, hugged her and they kissed.

"A porter," Vivien said. "We need a porter. These things weigh a ton."

She was tall, slender, and smart, in a nigger-brown suit with a short mink jacket over it, and with her black hair brushed sleekly off her face and coiled up simply at the back of her small head. She had never been wealthy, but always managed to look as if she were.

Christine shook her head. "The porters here always hide when trains come in. We'll have to manage by ourselves. Anyway, I managed to park right at the entrance."

They took a suitcase each and toiled along the platform with them.

"Barry sends his love and wishes he could have come too," Vivien went on. "To be honest, I'm glad he couldn't. I always feel a fool trying to give a talk when he's in the audience. He knows so much more than I do. Tell me, is this going to be a terribly intimidating affair tonight? I've brought an evening dress, as you said I'd got to, but it isn't at all grand. And I'm not going to talk for long—I *can't* talk for long, I just get muddled and nervous—but the collection of shoes I've borrowed from the Blanchland is quite exciting, and if I can't think of anything else to say, I can always chat on about them. Christine, it's marvellous seeing you again. I'm so looking forward to a couple of days of absolute peace and quiet. I'm worn out, absolutely worn out. And it's always so gloriously peaceful, staying with you and Henry. You're such peaceful people, somehow. The stress of modern living seems to have passed you by."

They went through the barrier and stowed the suitcases into the car and got into it.

"Perhaps," Christine said as they drove off, "I ought to have warned you that things may not be as peaceful as usual. We've my niece and nephew staying with us. My brother's children, Frances and David, ages seven and nine."

"Marvellous," Vivien said. "I adore children."

"And we've an *au pair* girl who's helping us look after them, and Mrs. Heacham—she was here when you came in the spring, wasn't she? And now her son's come to stay, and of course we've still got Mrs. Deeping, the policeman's wife, to do most of the cleaning."

Vivien looked blank for a moment, then exclaimed, "But it's a houseparty! Not at all what I expected." She began to laugh. "Oh, if you could see yourself! You ought to be on top of the world. You've got what every middle-class woman who paces along wearily behind her vacuum cleaner has daydreams about as she droops over her morning coffee. But you look as if something frightful had hit you."

"I'm not sure it hasn't," Christine said. "I can't explain it. I thought it would be wonderful myself. I thought I'd have time for all the things I've always wanted to do, paint a bit, take classes in dressmaking and make ravishing clothes, and do a bit more entertaining in a civilised way. But something doesn't feel right. Mrs. Heacham not only has a rather difficult temperament, but she's got an ulcer, or thinks she has, which means we can't eat anything she doesn't like. And we have to be absolutely punctual for meals, or she takes it as a deliberate insult to her cooking, and somehow I don't seem to have any more time than I had before."

"You'll get used to it," Vivien said. "Oh God, you don't know how quickly I could get used to it! But I've always had luxurious tastes. How d'you like my jacket?"

"Beautiful," Christine said.

Vivien's clothes always were. The evening dress which she had said might not be grand enough for that evening would probably make every other woman in the room look frumpish.

"Actually I bought it secondhand from a rich friend who'd taken a dislike to it," Vivien said. "Wouldn't you love to be able to afford dislikes like that? But working in a museum has an odd way of bringing you in contact with some surprisingly rich people. But you know, one of the reasons I love Barry so is that he panders to my love of luxury. Actually the jacket didn't cost *nothing*, if you see what I mean. And both Alec and Miles used to make me feel sinful for liking nice things. But Barry understands how much lovely textures mean to me, and scents and flavours. They're just as important to him too. The only thing that's wrong with him is that he isn't a millionaire. But we scrape along. I wish I'd met him when I was young! I'd have turned into a different sort of person."

They chatted on until they reached the house.

At the door Christine said, "We may as well take these

things straight up to your room, then we can have some tea."

She took one of the bags and pushed the door open. Vivien followed her with the second bag.

They went upstairs to the spare room, the door of which was ajar. Christine pushed it open.

Something fell on her head.

Because she was startled, it took her a moment to realise what it was. It was something not very heavy, which, as it bumped off her forehead, released a spurt of cold water over her, then made a wet stain on the carpet just inside the door.

It was a booby trap, of course, put there by the children. An old soup tin, filled with water, had been balanced on the top of the door, waiting for her and Vivien.

The children plainly did not feel in the least guilty about it, for as they came bounding out of their room, they stood on the landing, doubled up with laughter.

"Luckily for you I'm wearing my head scarf," Christine said, "or the hair-do I had for the dinner would have suffered, and I shouldn't have taken that too well."

Unknotting the scarf, she mopped her face and neck with it, and tried not to show too much irritation. She did not like practical jokes. Most of the satisfaction to be got from them, she thought, was sadistic. In adults they seemed to her absolutely unforgiveable. But even quite nice children seemed to have to go through a phase when booby traps, and hiding things that were going to be wanted, and making apple-pie beds struck them as the height of humour. Her theory about these tricks was that the best way to treat them, if one's self-control were up to the job, was to let them quietly misfire.

Pointing to the empty tin, she added, "Take that thing away, David." Then she went on into the bedroom, put down Vivien's suitcase and said to her, "Come down for tea when you're ready."

Vivien had stayed still on the landing, looking as if she were afraid that something else might fall if she came through the doorway.

"But that was meant for *me!*" she said. It seemed that she thought this the most serious aspect of the incident.

"Well, luckily it missed you." Christine turned to go downstairs.

"Do you mean to say you're going to let them get away with it?" Vivien asked.

"If you mean, am I going to let myself get worked up about a little water," Christine said, "no, it isn't worth it."

"That's the way to spoil children," Vivien said. "All this permissiveness is simply laziness on the part of their parents."

"I expect it is," Christine said, "only I'm not a parent of theirs, and if I do some irremediable damage to their characters while they're here, that's just too bad."

"I'd at least make them apologise," Vivien said.

"All right," said Christine. "David, apologise."

"Who to?" he asked.

"To both of us," she said. "You meant the water for Mrs. Richmond, and it got me. You owe each of us an apology."

"Why just me?" David said. "Why not Frances too?"

"We'll come to Frances in a minute. But you thought of it, didn't you?"

"Yes," he admitted.

"But I helped," Frances said brightly. "I held the tin while he climbed on the chair."

"I haven't heard that apology yet," Vivien said acidly.

David gave her a lowering look and muttered, "I'm sorry."

"That's not what I'd call gracious," she said.

"I'm sorry, I'm sorry, I'm sorry!" he suddenly yelled at her and bolted into the room from which he and Frances had emerged.

Frances, believing in his vast superiority to most of the human race, inevitably copied him, though in a gay and lighthearted tone. "I'm sorry, I'm sorry, I'm sorry!" Then she also disappeared into their room, and the door closed on her with a slam.

Vivien advanced into the spare room.

"I'm sorry too," she said. "I know it's quite shocking to interfere with the way other people see fit to bring up their children. I'll just have a wash now, then I'd love that tea you mentioned."

"They aren't my children," Christine said, "and I'm not bringing them up, I'm simply trying to survive them."

"They're very charming really," Vivien went on. "So open. No pretending they hadn't played that silly trick. So honest about it. I oughtn't to have flared up. But I'm always edgey when I've a thing like this dinner ahead of me. I'm all right once I get started. I even rather enjoy putting on the performance. But I'm always nervous beforehand. I suppose those children will hate me now and I do so dislike being hated. I'll have to be extra nice to them. Do they like chocolates? I brought some for you, but if it'll help to make peace, I'll say they were meant for them."

She opened one of the suitcases and took out a box of chocolates, tied up with pink satin ribbon.

"For God's sake, no," Christine said. "A slap with one hand and a caress with the other, that's the one thing I know one mustn't try. Consistency's the important thing. So I'll keep the chocolates, if I may, and thank you very much."

Vivien repeated that she would be down for tea in a few minutes, and Christine left her.

While she and Henry were waiting for Vivien to come down, Marsha brought the tea into the sitting room. Christine told her and Henry about the soup tin and the water.

"Water," he said. "I think that shows a nice disposition. It could so easily have been paint, which would have done some real damage."

Christine thought of paint all over Vivien's lovely secondhand mink jacket and said a heartfelt, "Thank God they didn't think of it!"

"Oh, I don't think they'd have used paint, even if they'd thought of it," Marsha said. "I'm sure Mr. Findon's right, they're much too nice, they aren't at all malicious."

"But I'll speak to them," Henry said. "It's not the way to treat guests. About this affair tonight, I suppose I've really got to get into a dinner jacket, haven't I? There's no way out?"

Christine had known that this would come up sooner or later. Henry never put on a dinner jacket without making at least a token protest, while if it happened to be tails that he had to wear, the protest was from the heart and desperate. On those occasions Christine always dressed as early as she could and got out of his way, leaving their bedroom to him as a lonely battlefield.

"You've not only got to wear a dinner jacket," she said, "but you've got to be ready by six o'clock, because the Maskells are coming in for drinks." She had told him this before, of course, but knew that it was just as well to remind him.

As she had expected, he said, "The Maskells?" in a wondering voice, as if they were not among the Findons' oldest friends in Helsington.

"For drinks," she repeated distinctly. "At six o'clock."

"What a business," Henry said dispiritedly. "Why does one do these things? Wouldn't it be much nicer to have the evening to ourselves?"

This happened almost every time that he and Christine went out. A week or so before the occasion, Henry was capable of believing that he would enjoy it, and when he was actually in the middle of it he enjoyed it as much as anyone, but in the few hours before it a deep gloom settled on him at the prospect of being torn away from his home. There had been a time when Christine had taken this seriously, but now she let his grumbles wash past her, pretending that she had not heard them.

"Rodney's coming over for drinks," she said to Marsha, "but of course not going on to the dinner."

Marsha said, "Oh," and appeared not to be interested.

Rodney was the Maskells' son, of just Marsha's age, and at their first meeting had shown obvious signs of instant infatuation. Christine was not sure what Marsha's response had been. She had listened to him with her sweet, grave attentiveness, and laughed kindly at his jokes. But then, she did the same with everybody. She had also been out with him two or three times, but had never appeared any more excited by this than by going for a drive with the children. On the whole, Christine was inclined to feel sorry for Rodney and to hope that the emotion that had hit him did not go too deep. He was a pleasant young man, rather shy and solemn and probably easily hurt. He was studying to become a chartered accountant and spent most of the week in London, but usually came home for the weekends. If Marsha wanted him to stay on this evening when everyone else had gone to the dinner, he would only too eagerly agree. But Christine was leaving that to Marsha. If, in fact, he bored her, Christine did not want to make her suffer more of him than she wanted.

Christine was drawing the curtains when Vivien came into the room. The dusk was closing in and with it a few raindrops had spattered the glass of the window. Standing looking out for a moment, Christine saw that Lew Heacham had swept the leaves up from the lawn and made a small bonfire of them at the far end of the garden. She could still see a red glow in the heap as it smouldered on. But the rain, if it persisted, would soon put it out, she thought.

Vivien and Henry kissed, he introduced Marsha, then Vivien dropped into a chair and gave a great sigh. Taking the cup of tea that Henry brought her, she said, "I think I'll have a rest before I change. You don't mind, do you? I'll just lie down for half an hour. I'm nearly dead." Suddenly she seemed to become fully aware of Marsha, instead of barely noticing her, as she had when they were introduced. She stared at her as if silenced and somehow put out by the girl's beauty. Yet Vivien had never had any reason to envy another woman her beauty, and she always claimed that youth was something that she was glad to have left behind her.

Marsha smiled at her, but Vivien did not respond. She went on looking at Marsha in a curiously blank way, almost as if she felt that she had met the girl before, but could not remember where or when. Then, as if deliberately dismissing whatever she had on her mind, she remarked, "Your curtains are new since I was here last. I like them. What time do we have to leave this evening?"

"Not till about ten past seven," Christine said, "but we've some friends coming in for drinks at six, then they're going to drive us on to the Crown." The Crown was the restaurant where the dinner was to be held. "So you'll arrive there in state. They've a Bentley."

Vivien glanced at her watch, as if calculating how long she had for her rest.

"Who are they—these friends?" she asked.

"Minna and Tony Maskell," Christine said. "Minna's secretary of the society. In fact she's the person who really keeps it going."

"She's a chronic committeewoman," Henry said. "She keeps half the things that happen in Helsington going."

"And she's got a marvellous collection of Victorian mourning jewellery," Christine said. "A really fine one. If you'd like to, we could probably go over to them tomorrow and see it."

"Do you know what I'd really like to do tomorrow?" Vivien said. "Absolutely nothing at all. Just sit around and gossip. Couldn't we do that?"

"Of course," Christine said. "I just didn't want you to be bored."

"I shan't be bored. I'm so *tired* . . . What does Mr. Maskell do?"

"Manufactures kitchen plastics."

"Oh, *that* Maskell. I've got loads of Maskellware myself. Then I suppose he's frightfully rich." A look of interest kindled on her face for a moment, but it faded almost at once. She finished her tea, put down the cup and stood up. "Well, I'll be down at six. But now I've simply got to have a rest, or I'll make a horrid hash of things this evening."

She went out.

Henry looked after her with a worried frown. "What's the matter with her, Christine? She doesn't usually go in for being so tired. She isn't ill, is she?"

"She hasn't said so, and she doesn't look it," Christine answered.

"I hope it isn't trouble with Barry," he said. "If a third marriage goes on the rocks, I really don't know what you do next."

"If three marriages go wrong," Marsha said austerely, "then there's something the matter with you. You probably ought never to have married at all."

"She was talking very affectionately about him, coming back from the station," Christine said. "I shouldn't think it's that."

"I think, if you marry," Marsha went on, "it should be for always. I don't think all this starting and stopping is at all right."

"But suppose you make a mistake," Christine said.

"You shouldn't make mistakes."

"And just how are you going to avoid it?"

"You and Mr. Findon must know much more about it than I do," Marsha answered. "You didn't make a mistake, did you?"

"That was just luck," Henry said. "There's an awful lot of luck involved. Just think how few people you meet in life of the right sex, the right age group and even remotely the right qualifications. It's sheer chance if you pick on someone you're going to be able to endure for the rest of your life."

"But if you really *love* someone . . ." Marsha paused and her cheeks went pink. "Of course, I know you're laughing at me, but I do think your generation are perfectly awful about marriage. You don't seem to think it means anything."

"We aren't laughing," Henry said. In fact he was far too accustomed to the solemnities of the young ever to laugh at them. "But the press and television keep telling us that it's your generation that don't take marriage seriously."

"I know, it's very unfair," she said. "One's only got to sit quietly listening to some middle-aged people talking, and what do they talk about? Divorce, divorce, divorce. I think it's terrible. When I marry—I mean, *if* I marry, and I may not want to, because I quite see your point about how chancey it is, meeting someone you can stand—but if I do, it's going to last."

"At least, that's a good approach," Henry said. "And I hope you have luck."

"Of course, I'm not talking about extra-marital sex," she said.

"Oh," he said, "you're not."

"No, I think it's quite insane to marry someone you haven't slept with."

"Ah," he said.

"Well, don't you?"

"Luck comes in, even then," he replied evasively.

She looked quickly from him to Christine and the pink in her cheeks deepened. "I'm sorry, I wasn't suggesting— I mean, I wasn't asking . . ."

Christine, grinning, said, "Well, I'm going to go and get dressed." She thought that as Henry had allowed himself to be inveigled into this age-old discussion, she might as well leave him to extricate himself how ever he could.

Going upstairs, she decided to look in on the children.

She found a scene of touching peace in their room, the room that had been given to them as a playroom, though they often preferred to use other rooms for their occupations. Their bedroom was a floor higher, between Marsha's and Mrs. Heacham's, in what Mrs. Heacham always referred to as the attics, as if she had been banished to some dark, draughty roof space. In fact, the rooms up there were big and light and cheerful.

Lew was with the children now. He and Frances were doing a jigsaw puzzle together. They sat facing each other across a small table on which all the pieces were spread out, near to the gas fire. Both were silent and absorbed. At the bigger table in the middle of the room, David was sitting writing. He was writing with a ballpoint pen in an exercise book, sitting in a curiously hunched position, with one arm curled round the book as if he were taking precautions against what he was slowly and thoughtfully writing being read by anyone else. As soon as he saw Christine, he jerked the arm across the page, to hide it completely, and scowled at her. It was only when he was sure that she was not going to try to read what he had written, that he relaxed and quietly closed the exercise book.

"Christine, I *am* sorry about the water," he said earnestly. "It was awfully silly."

"It was, just a bit," she agreed.

"It was all my fault," he said. "Frances only did what I told her."

Frances took no notice of them, being occupied in trying to force a jagged piece of the jigsaw into a space clearly not intended for it. Lew reached out and gently took it away from her.

"Not there, love—here," he said.

"Oo!" she murmured admiringly. "That's clever. It's part of the lady's dress."

"You seem to be good with children," Christine said to Lew.

"I like being with them," he said. "You know where you are with them. No need to put on a show. No, that isn't what I mean. I mean . . ." He hesitated. "Well, if you do a bit of pretending, they understand you. Nobody gets hurt. I used to do a lot of pretending when I was a kid, and got called a liar for it."

"You *are* a bit of a liar, Lew," David said. "But it's all right, I won't tell."

Lew laughed self-consciously. "I've been telling them a few yarns," he said. "They always see through me."

David gave a chuckle. "Shall I tell you what I'm doing?" he said to Christine. "I'm writing a novel."

"That sounds impressive," she said. "Am I going to be allowed to read it?"

"No, no, no!" he cried with swift anxiety, and clutched the exercise book to his breast. "Nobody's ever going to read it, nobody ever!"

"Aren't novels written to be read?" she asked.

"Not mine!" he said with passion. "If you try to read it, I'll kill you, that's what I'll do! I will, I'll kill you! You're never to look at it."

"Now is that a nice sort of thing to say?" Lew said, catching Christine's eye and smiling. "To Mrs. Findon, of all people."

David relaxed a little as he saw that no one was going to snatch his book from him.

"Of course, I don't mean *kill* you," he said reassuringly.

"I was hoping you didn't," Christine said. "I'm not really ready to die."

Frances had got up and twined her arms round Lew's waist.

"You tell her," she said. "Go on, tell her."

"Tell her what?" he said.

"That you aren't going away tomorrow. You aren't, are you? You promised you'd stay."

He smiled at Christine again, rather uneasily, but he spoke to Frances. "I didn't, you know. I just said, we'll see. You can't stay in a place if you haven't been invited."

"If you want to stay on, Lew, that's quite all right," Christine said, "Henry would like it. He was very glad to see you again. So really it depends on your mother."

"That's very kind of you," he said. "I'm very grateful. But what my mother wants . . . You know, I've never known what she wanted. D'you suppose she ever has herself? Except that she must have wanted to be old Mr. Findon's housekeeper, or she wouldn't have stayed with him so long. In a way, I expect she's felt like a kind of widow ever since he died. And I'd like to help her, if only I knew how, but I don't seem able to say anything right. It's obvious it would have been better if I'd stayed away."

"Give her a little time," Christine said. "You can't expect to walk back into her life all of a sudden and have everything just the same as it was before you went away. She's got to punish you at least a little for what you made her suffer."

His face tightened. "She wasn't the only one who suffered. If I hadn't got away from her—yes, and the rest of them too—I'd never have grown up into a real person."

"Well, as I told you, you're very welcome," Christine said. "Don't let your mother make you hide from us."

"Thank you. If you mean that . . ."

"I do."

"Well then, I'll stay a few days anyway, and see if Mum and I can come to terms."

"Good." She meant it, mainly because she knew that the rather sad story of the pallid little boy living unhappily and almost secretly in his father's home had always distressed Henry, and this seemed to be a chance to lay that ghost. But at the same time she wondered if six months hence they might not find that they had a living-in handyman-cum-baby-sitter added to their already inflated staff. Saying that she had to go and dress, Christine left them.

It did not take her long to change into her evening dress and silver slippers. Both dress and slippers were about three years old. She had to wear evening dress only about twice a year, so when she bought one it always lasted her until she had the feeling that she could not bear the thought of being seen in it ever again. She was getting near that state with her present one, but she still had a faint liking for it. It was of dark blue silk jersey with a silver belt. Zipping it up, she put on her seed-pearl earrings and necklace to match, put what she needed into her evening bag, and went downstairs again, leaving the bedroom free for Henry to create havoc in as he changed into his dinner jacket.

Putting her head into the sitting room, she told him that the field was clear, then she went out to the kitchen to tell Mrs. Heacham that there was no need for her to send Lew away if she would like him to stay on for a little.

But the kitchen was empty. Mrs. Heacham must already have gone up to her room. She always went to bed early, taking her supper of milk and an egg with her on a tray, leaving the dishing-up of dinner to Marsha. Tonight Mrs. Heacham had gone up rather earlier than she generally did, but no doubt she had been upset by Lew's arrival.

But she had performed the nightly ritual of locking up before she went. The catch on the window was fastened and the back door was bolted. Every evening, before she went to bed, she made a round of the ground-floor rooms, making sure that every window was securely latched, and that the front door was on its chain. And if by any chance Henry and Christine went out and forgot to fasten the chain when they came in, she always lectured them next morning. It was not fair on the police, she told them, not to take adequate precautions. Of course they agreed with her. She was perfectly right. Yet it gave both of them an uncomfortably claustrophobic feeling to see her going round from room to room, turning their house nightly into a fortress.

The chain on the front door was in place tonight, which was absurd, because Mrs. Heacham knew that they were going out. But it was by such small, persevering acts of self-assertion that she made her presence constantly felt.

Naturally, Christine had to remove the chain now because the Maskells were coming.

She heard their ring at about ten minutes past six. Henry had not reappeared yet, nor had Vivien. Rodney Maskell came in behind his parents, as silent as usual, with his glance going straight past Christine to the open door of the sitting room to see if Marsha were there. He was a stocky young man with wide shoulders, a rather short neck, a round head and a round, slightly childish-looking face, from the high forehead of which, however, the smooth fair hair was already receding. He was sensitive about this, and tried to brush it so that this early baldness did not show. His eyes, large and brown and intelligent, with long dark lashes, were his best feature. They were very like his mother's, though in her face they were embedded in folds of rosy, dimpled flesh. She was a stout little woman, who looked almost cylindrical from her shoulders to the hem of her dress, which this evening was a glittering mass of golden sequins. She was wearing some of her famous mourning jewellery with it, gold, with decorations on it in diamonds and jet. Her hair had a steel-grey rinse and was puffed out round her head with a great deal of back-combing. Her voice had the clear resonance of the experienced committeewoman.

"Those pearls, those lovely pearls—I'm so glad you're wearing them!" she exclaimed, embracing Christine warmly, and pretending not to recognise her dress, even after its long past, told her how much she liked it. Then she went with her usual little trotting steps into the sitting room and cried, "This room—I adore it! It's so wonderfully peaceful. Those are new curtains, aren't they? My dear, how clever you are, you always get things just right. Tony, isn't she clever? Every time I come here, I say to myself I'll go home and change absolutely everything. But it's no good, even when I do, my taste's incurably bad. Tony, isn't my taste hopeless?"

Tony gave a little giggle and said, "Hopeless, yes, hopeless. Very clever, Christine, very clever."

He nearly always giggled before saying anything. He was hardly taller than his wife, but unlike her, was a wizened little figure, who always looked as if he had shrunk slightly in the last wash, leaving his good clothes fractionally too big for him all over. Both he and Minna were people of formidable energy and unbending determination, but of immense friendliness too. They had taken to Henry and Christine, she sometimes felt, simply because they were about as unlike them as they could possibly be. Certainly that was one of the reasons why the Findons liked the Maskells as much as they did. They made a very bracing change from schoolmasters and schoolmasters' wives.

Rodney had followed them into the room and was standing looking at Marsha in a stupor of admiration. She was aware of it, but pretended not to be and started moving about the room, fluffing up cushions and removing books and papers from chairs. Although Henry had a study all to himself, his books and papers strayed all over the rest of the house.

Christine started to pour out drinks, but as Henry appeared he took the job over from her.

"And where's our distinguished visitor?" Minna asked. She sat bolt upright in one of the comfortable chairs, with her little legs stuck out straight, because her girdle would not have let her relax. "Shoes happen to be something I'm particularly interested in. You know we've been making a collection of china ones. So interesting. The early ones go back to the seventeenth century, and of course they continue through Victorian times, and some of them are enchantingly pretty. Aren't they, Tony?"

He giggled and said, "Make good ashtrays too—yes, very pretty."

Henry looked at his watch and said, "I suppose Vivien isn't asleep. She said she was so tired. I wonder if someone ought to go up and make sure."

"I'll go," Marsha said.

But as she said it, the door was flung open. Vivien stood there. She wore a white dress with flecks of gold in it and long gold earrings. Her black hair was sleek and shining. Her eyes and her cheeks were brilliant. She looked very beautiful and very dramatic, but unluckily that brilliance of eye and cheek was the burning glow of rage. She was holding up her skirt in front, so that they could all see that she had on one golden sandal, but that on her other foot she had only a stocking.

"Those damned kids!" she screamed. "They've taken all my shoes! All my *left* shoes! Every single damned one of them! And how am I going to go and talk at your dinner now? Every one of my left shoes has been stolen!"

# 3

Henry said, "I don't understand—what's happened, Vivien?"

She came into the room, walking with a limp because of the heel on her one sandal.

"They've stolen my shoes," she repeated.

"Those shoes from the Blanchland?" Minna cried in horror. Christine instantly had a vision of damages to be paid because of the loss of the collection, or because of some slight harm that might have come to some valuable item in it. At the same moment she had an overlapping vision of an evening ruined, Vivien too angry to say her piece, perhaps even to go to the dinner at all, and all of it in some way Christine's responsibility, because it had been her idea that Vivien should be invited.

"No, no, no!" Vivien answered, her voice rising with each word. "My own shoes. All my left shoes. I haven't a single pair to wear except the ones I came in."

"And you think the children took them?" Henry went on. Then he remembered that he had not introduced Vivien to the Maskells, and quietly did so.

She gave them a brief nod then glared again at Henry.

"Of course they did. Who else would play a silly trick like that? They've tried to play one trick on me already, and it's just chance it misfired. But I showed them what I thought of it, so they've taken their revenge."

"Just how many pairs of shoes did you bring?" Christine asked. After all, Vivien was staying only till Monday.

"These evening sandals," she said, "and a pair of walking shoes, in case we went into the country tomorrow, and my bedroom slippers, and my patent leather pumps, in case you were giving a party of any sort tomorrow, that's all. And now the ones I arrived in are the only ones I've got left, and I can't possibly wear them with this dress."

"And it's only the left shoes they've taken?" Henry said. "It seems an odd sort of trick to play."

"It's nasty and malicious," Vivien said fiercely.

"It is rather," he agreed, "if they really did it."

"Well, who else in this house would do it?" she demanded. "Who else would do something so silly, just to make me look like a fool and spoil my evening. I don't know of anyone here who's got anything special against me."

"When do you think it happened?" Minna Maskell asked, her voice clear and firm, as if she had decided that it was about time for her to take charge. "When did they have access to your belongings?"

Vivien looked faintly surprised at the tone of authority that had issued from the plump little woman in the glittering dress.

"I suppose while we were having tea," she said. "That's the only time my room's been empty. I went up there straight afterwards for a rest, and I've been there ever since. And I only realised the shoes were gone when I'd finished changing and was going to put these sandals on. Then I saw they'd all gone, all the left ones."

Minna went on, "Were the children alone at that time, I wonder. Marsha, my dear, I suppose you weren't with them?"

Tony gave a little giggle and said, "An alibi! That's it, Henry, find out if they've got an alibi. Trust Minna to go to the heart of the matter."

"As a matter of fact, I was in my room," Marsha said, "working on some lecture notes. I don't know what they were doing."

"Well, wait a minute, will you, Vivien?" Henry said.

"If the children took the shoes we can obviously sort the matter out fairly easily. Don't worry."

He went out and they heard him going upstairs.

Dropping into a chair, crossing her knees with her long skirt pulled up so that it showed her shoeless foot swinging in the air, Vivien said, "It's really ridiculous, isn't it, to be made helpless by a pair of children like that? And how to explain to other people what happened . . .!"

Marsha said, "I was wondering—they aren't as nice as yours, but I've got some gold evening shoes. If you'd care to borrow them . . ."

Vivien took a swift look at Marsha's feet. "That's very sweet of you, but . . ." She thrust her own foot forward to compare it with Marsha's. Vivien's foot was slender and elegant, but undoubtedly very much longer than Marsha's. "Not a hope, is there?"

"I've some old silver ones," Christine said, "but they'd be much too broad for you."

"Now let's all just keep our heads," Minna said. "Henry will probably return with all the shoes. I adore David and Frances, and I can't see them doing something so very mean as refusing to say where they've put the shoes. As soon as Henry explains to them how much it matters, they'll give them back. And if they don't—well, it's no good my offering Mrs. Richmond my shoes, though I'd gladly do so, because my feet are *very* small—but we'll think of some solution. The main thing is not to let ourselves get flustered and spoil what I know is going to be a simply wonderful evening. Meanwhile, Christine dear, Mrs. Richmond hasn't got a drink. In her place, I think I'd be wild for one. It isn't just the shoes, but she's going to speak to us, and I myself always need at least two good strong drinks before I address an audience. And the drinks at the dinner, as we all know, will be on the meagre side. One simply can't supply the sort of drinks one should unless one raises the price for the affair rather above what a good many of our members can afford. So don't let's take Mrs. Richmond away without sufficient alcohol in her bloodstream."

Christine gave Minna a look of gratitude. It was fantastic of her, of course, to say that she could not address an audience without having had two strong drinks. In fact, she could jump to her little feet and address any audience on anything whatever at ten seconds' warning. But a drink would certainly be good for Vivien, and with Henry leaving before he had poured one out for her, Christine had not thought of taking over from him.

She asked Vivien now what she would like and Vivien asked for whisky. Christine poured it out and took it to her as Henry reappeared, followed by David, Frances, and Lew. Henry came right into the room, David and Frances stayed in the doorway, and Lew hovered in the hall behind them.

"They say," Henry said, his innocent-seeming glance on Vivien's face, his tone mild and unruffled, which to Christine meant that he was actually fairly seriously disturbed, "that they didn't take your shoes."

Her temper blazed again. "Of course they did! They're liars too, are they? I'd be willing to forgive them for a silly trick, if they said they were sorry, but a liar I cannot stand!"

"We aren't liars," David said in a tone so soft and calm that it sounded curiously like Henry's. In fact, he might have been deliberately parodying Henry. He had a certain talent as a mimic. "Are we, Frances?"

"No, we aren't," she said.

"So it's silly to say we are, Mrs. Richmond, it won't help you to get your silly old shoes," David went on, still in Henry's voice, and he gave her a gentle, confiding smile.

To Christine there was something startling and almost frightening about that smile. It was so condescending. It was so mature. At the same time, it was somehow sly. She had never noticed any slyness in the children before. Usually they had a disarming way of admitting any offence that they might have committed, of apologising and immediately assuming, with sunny confidence, that all was well now. That smile convinced her that David had taken the shoes, even if Frances knew nothing about it, and that it was not going to be easy to get them back.

"Listen, David," she said, "this isn't a joke, it's serious. We've all got to go out soon, and Mrs. Richmond needs her gold shoe to go out in. There isn't time to play Hunt the Slipper. What have you done with it?"

His gaze and the strange smile moved to her. "But I told you, Christine, I never touched it."

"Lew," Henry said, "were you up there with the children while we were having tea?"

Lew hesitated. After a moment he said, "Matter of fact, no, I was having tea with Mum. I only went up to them when we finished."

"No, he wasn't with us," Frances said serenely. "We were all by ourselves. We were having a private talk."

"Silly!" David said to her acidly. "A talk isn't private if you tell everyone what it's about."

"And what *was* it about?" Vivien asked. "About how to steal my shoes?"

His gaze, bland, secretive, deeply amused, slid back to her. He was hugging some joke to himself that he did not mean to share with any of them.

"I didn't steal your shoes," he said. "I don't steal."

"Borrow them, then," she said, making an unusual effort to keep her patience.

"I didn't borrow them either."

"Do you know who did?" Henry asked.

It was beginning to sound like a guessing game.

"No," David said.

"And I always thought you were such a nice boy," Minna Maskell said, "and here you are, being perfectly horrid."

"The main problem is time," Henry said. "I can deal with David later, but here and now, since he isn't going to tell us where the shoes are, we've got to think out what Vivien can do."

"I could have just a quick look round for the shoes first," Marsha suggested.

Perhaps she thought that if she could take David away from his audience, and particularly from Vivien, she might get the truth out of him.

Henry said, "Good idea," and Christine said, "I'll help—you take upstairs and I'll take down." They went out, Marsha shepherding David and Frances ahead of her.

But ten minutes later Marsha and Christine were back in the sitting room, with nothing achieved. Christine had looked in the kitchen and the storeroom, though she did not see how David could have hidden the shoes there, since Mrs. Heacham and Lew would have been having tea in the kitchen at the time when the shoes disappeared, and when they had finished tea Lew had joined the children upstairs. She had looked in the dining room, in Henry's study and the cupboard under the stairs. Marsha said that she had looked rapidly through the bedrooms and cupboards upstairs, and had tried to persuade David to tell her what he had done with the shoes, but that he had only repeated that he had not touched them.

"Well, the important thing to decide at the moment," Minna said, "is what Mrs. Richmond's going to wear to this dinner. You're sure, Mrs. Richmond, you can't face the idea of wearing the shoes you came in?"

Vivien gave a sigh and said, "I will, if I absolutely must. I don't want to let everybody down. Anyway, at a dinner, one's feet are under the table most of the time. Yes, all right, I'll do that."

Tony Maskell, with his little titter, said, "Splendid, splendid, that's the spirit!"

From the doorway, Lew said, "I know what I'd do, if I were Mrs. Richmond."

Until then, Vivien had barely noticed him. She looked round at him now, took in his finely modelled features, his well-shaped head, his smiling charm. She smiled.

"What would you do?" she asked.

"I'd wear the one golden slipper," he said, "and I'd put a bandage on the other foot, and borrow a bedroom slipper from someone—you could get it to fit well enough by the way you arrange the bandage—and, if you can, I'd borrow a stick—a nice, elegant cane with a silver handle would be best—then I'd walk with a very slight limp and tell people how you twisted your ankle getting out of a taxi. And everyone will sympathise with you and think how enormously brave and conscientious of you it was to turn up at all, and you won't feel at all grotesque, as you would if you were wearing your other shoes with that dress."

They all began to laugh, all except Vivien, who looked steadily at Lew for a moment, then exclaimed, "Genius! Quick—find me a bandage and a slipper!"

"Oh, for God's sake, Vivien!" Christine said. "You don't mean to do it!"

"I do, I do!" She got quickly to her feet. "A bandage and a slipper. It's the perfect answer. It's important. Don't you understand, I'm going to be talking about shoes—about fashion in shoes, their elegance, their workmanship, the kind of clothes they went with? Just think how I'd feel if the ones I was wearing myself were utterly wrong. Lew, you're brilliant."

He looked a little surprised at the enthusiasm with which she had taken up his suggestion. He had probably not meant it to be taken seriously. But naturally he did not mind being told that he was brilliant. Christine, accepting the situation, took Vivien upstairs to look for a crêpe bandage and for a bedroom slipper for her to wear with it, while Henry, beginning to be amused, or at least doing what he could to get Vivien's mind off David and his iniquity, said that he thought that there was a cane somewhere in the storeroom, and went to look for it. When Christine and Vivien came downstairs again, with Vivien's ankle bandaged, he met them with a slim black cane with an ivory handle, which had sometimes been used by his father during the last years of his life.

Vivien took the cane and posed for them, leaning on it, a restrained look of suffering on her face. She had always had a love of the histrionic. Then she burst out laughing.

"Now I'd enjoy that second drink that Mrs. Maskell so sensibly said I ought to have," she said, and practicing her limp, returned to her chair in the sitting room.

They left the house at ten minutes past seven in the Maskells' Bentley. The rain that had been in the air all day had come at last, only a light, misty drizzle, but it made the evening far colder than the earlier part of the day. Tony Maskell drove. Rodney had stayed behind, perhaps to be given a meal, along with Lew and the children, by Marsha, or perhaps to find that he would have to walk home through the rain. Christine did not inquire what Marsha had in mind for him. The Maskells' house, in any case, was not very far away. It was a big Victorian house on the outskirts of

Helsington, expensively modernized and surrounded by about an acre of beautifully kept garden. Rodney could reach it in a quarter of an hour and if Marsha had not been hospitable, would not be allowed to starve by the Portuguese couple who ran the house.

The Crown, where the dinner was to be held, was in the main street of Helsington, a characterless street, except for the Crown itself, which was a nice old inn, and the really splendid Elizabethan Town Hall. The other buildings were mainly Woolworth's, Marks and Spencer's, Boot's, and C. & A., and a crop of boutiques, which failed and were reopened by new owners so quickly that Christine had stopped trying to keep count of them.

In the daytime the parking along the street was so dense that no one in his senses bothered to look for a place there, but in the evenings it was usually fairly empty. Tony stopped in front of the Crown, so that the rest of the party could get out there, and while Vivien, accompanied solicitously by Minna, Henry, and Christine, limped pathetically across the pavement to the entrance, her lips taut with pain, he went on and parked a little way down the street. When he joined the others, they went up in the lift to the dining room on the first floor.

At dinner they had smoked salmon, duck in orange sauce, and ice cream with fruit salad. It was the meal that the Crown laid on for every function held there, unless its organisers took a strong line from the start, and would face a sharp rise in price. The Findons, the Maskells, and, of course, Vivien, were at the top table, which meant that they had a sharp draught down their necks from the row of windows behind them, a frequent hazard of sitting at top tables. Vivien sat next to Arthur Winslow, Chairman of the Costume Society, a slender, erect man of about sixty, with thick grey hair, carefully brushed off his face in flat waves, which, with only a little use of the imagination, it was easy to imagine as a tie wig, topping his sharp, chiseled and lively features. When Christine saw him chatting to Vivien, helping her to unpack her collection of shoes and arrange them on a table, where she could reach them when she wanted to talk about them, she thought how distinguished he would look in a pair of such shoes as the one that he was delicately handling now. It was made of green silk damask, and had a high red heel and a silver buckle. Vivien had not brought its pair. With a start, Christine realised that, allowing for the fact that some of the earlier shoes were made without left or right, so that they could be worn on either foot, there were no left shoes . . .

A coincidence?

There is something curiously moving, curiously personal, about old shoes. Their wearers have left their mark upon them forever. With every wrinkle in the leather or cloth, with the wearing down of a heel or the breaking of a buckle, some man or woman out of the far past still lays claim to ownership. It brings that past into a very close and living relationship with us.

Besides the splendid green silk damask shoe with the red heel, Vivien had brought an intriguing collection with her. There was a lady's boot of royal blue linen, with square-cut, black patent leather toecaps. There was an exquisitely dainty little shoe of white satin, with ribbon stitched across it and ribbons to tie round the ankle, very like a modern ballet shoe. There were two Wellington boots, nothing like the clumping things called by that name now, but both very stylish, one of fine brown leather, the other consisting of a sort of black patent leather galosh, with a black ribbon bow on it, attached to a black silk stocking leg. It was designed, Vivien explained later, to be worn under trousers and look like a shoe and stocking. There were patterns too on the table, those oddly constructed iron contraptions into which the shoe could be slipped when the wearer wanted to go out walking on muddy roads. Also Vivien had brought some paste buckles with her, which gleamed attractively on the green baize cloth that covered the table.

At the end of the dinner the chairman rose and made a little speech, introducing Vivien, saying how heroic of her it had been to come when she had a badly sprained ankle, and suggesting that she should talk sitting down. But smiling bravely, she replied that she would prefer to stand, got to her feet and started.

She gave good value. First she spoke generally, then she

began picking up shoe after shoe from the table behind her,
dating it, describing the kind of clothes with which it would
have been worn, making her audience see ladies and gentle-
men in silks and satins moving among them, some with
corns and aching feet and some young and going gaily and
excitedly to a dance. There was one huge, heavy black
shoe, very worn, which she said had belonged to a farmer
and that it was possible still to detect the traces of dried
manure upon it. She pointed out subtleties of workmanship,
some of it so fine that it put modern shoes to shame. She
was witty too, and in that casual-sounding way of hers
which was the product of much rehearsal, kept her audience
laughing a good deal of the time. By the end of it Christine
was very grateful to her. As she sat down to applause, she
caught her eye and smiled. Vivien gave her back an empty
stare. The charm had been switched off, and she was back
among troubles of her own, which surely must go much
deeper, Christine thought with surprise, than the irritating
loss of four shoes, which would probably be explained
tomorrow. Was it possible, after all, that something was
going wrong between her and Barry?

In the car on the way home Christine praised her for the
way that she had spoken and thanked her for it. There had,
of course, been a vote of thanks at the end of the dinner,
then they had circulated for a while, then Vivien had packed
the shoes away again in the suitcase in which she had
brought them, and Henry had carried it down to the Maskells' car. It was raining harder now and a blustery wind
had risen.

Minna had heard what Christine said to Vivien and added
her praise.

"Oh, I thought you were splendid, Mrs. Richmond. It
was a really memorable talk. Of course, I've always been
fascinated by the subject of shoes. Did I tell you, I've a
collection of china shoes at home? I wonder if you'd care
to look at them. Not that I suppose they'd be anything
special from the point of view of an expert like yourself.
But some of them are so charming. Christine, could you
and Henry bring Mrs. Richmond over for drinks before lunch

tomorrow, say about twelve o'clock? I do hope you can. Or have you something else fixed up already?"

They had nothing else fixed up. But Christine remembered that Vivien had explicitly stated in the afternoon that she would like to take the following day as quietly as possible. Christine also knew that Vivien detested having expert opinions wheedled out of her under the guise of social chitchat. She disliked it almost as much as a doctor dislikes it when someone pours out a description of his symptoms over a friendly drink. So Christine replied that in fact they had planned to drive out into the country next day, weather permitting.

"Oh well, if it rains, perhaps you can bring Mrs. Richmond over," Minna said. "And bring that lovely girl, Marsha, with you. That would cheer Roddie up. He needs a lot of cheering up these days. He just sits and glowers at anyone who isn't Marsha."

The Maskells would not come in for a last drink, but deposited Vivien and the Findons on their doorstep and drove off into the darkness.

The light was on in the hall when they entered the house. The slight clanking of the door chain, as Henry closed the door behind them, reminded Christine to fasten it. Henry went towards the stairs, taking the suitcase of shoes with him.

"I'll take these straight up to your room, shall I, Vivien?" he said.

Christine went to the sitting room. The door was ajar and there was a light inside. She wondered if Rodney Maskell had stayed on and was still there with Marsha, or if perhaps she had Lew with her. Or the light might have been left on accidentally. She opened the door.

Her brother-in-law, Simon, was lying flat on the long sofa. His eyes were shut. One of his hands trailed on the floor. For a moment, after she had taken a step through the doorway, he did not stir. He seemed to be sound asleep. Then all at once he came to himself and shot up on to his feet. He blinked at her with a look of wild surprise, as if he could not think what she was doing there, or why he was there himself. Then he wrapped his arms round her and kissed her long and hard.

"Well, well," Vivien said from behind Christine, "it almost looks as if you two *are* still in love. I've often wondered about that."

# 4

Simon let Christine go and said, "Vivien, in the category of bitches I have known, you come very near the top."

"I'm sure I do," she answered, sounding rather as if she took it for a compliment.

She and Simon had never liked each other.

He watched her hobble into the room.

"What's the matter with your foot?" he asked.

"A slight case of theft."

Vivien sat down, hitched up her skirt, peeled off her stocking and unrolled the bandage. Then she stretched out her foot and turned it this way and that, as if she were making sure that it really was uninjured.

Simon turned to Christine. "This is really very odd. What's the trouble?"

Because he was sleepy and confused, he looked more like Henry than he usually did. Usually he looked far the more alert, the more forceful, and his grey eyes had a harder, more penetrating gaze. He stood straighter too, and there was no grey in his brown hair. Also he dressed far better than Henry, which he could afford, because in recent years he had become wealthy. Christine had never quite understood what he did, but knew that he was something or other in a unit trust, and besides advising other people on how to get rich, had managed to do very nicely for himself. He was the same age as Christine, which was three years younger than Henry.

She told him about the mystery of Vivien's shoe.

He sat down on the sofa and roared with laughter. After a moment she joined in.

"It does seem funny now," she said. "At the time I was furious. And I'll get furious again if the shoes don't turn up tomorrow. They weren't exactly cheap."

"Whose idea was the bandage?" Simon asked. "It was very ingenious."

"Lew's," she answered.

"Lew's?"

"Mrs. Heacham's Louis," Christine said. "He's suddenly turned up."

"After all these years?"

"Yes."

"Just out of the blue, or did he write first and explain himself?"

"Just out of the blue."

Simon rubbed one side of his jaw and looked thoughtful.

"I see I'd better go and get a room at the Crown," he said. "With Vivien staying here, and Lew, and David and Frances, and that dream of loveliness who let me in, who I suppose is your *au pair* girl, you can't have room for me. I'm sorry—if I'd realised, I wouldn't have come."

"You can use that sofa, if you like," Christine said.

"No, don't bother," he answered. "I'll go to the Crown. Can I use the telephone? I'll just make sure they've got a room."

He used the telephone in Henry's study. But the Crown, which was more of a restaurant than an hotel, and had not many rooms, was full up, so Simon, returning, said that he would like to borrow the sofa after all.

Vivien stood up. She had taken off her gold sandal as well as the bedroom slipper that Christine had lent her, and so could walk straight.

"I'm off to bed," she said. "Good night, Christine. Good night, Simon. If those shoes don't turn up . . ." She hesitated, as if she did not know what she would do then.

"We'll replace them," Christine said. "It's the least we can do."

She thought dismally of how expensive they had all certainly been.

"Don't be silly, that isn't what I was going to say." Vivien paused in the doorway. "Oh, never mind. I've at least got a whole pair of shoes to wear in the daytime."

She went out.

There was a silence between Simon and Christine, a faintly uneasy one, as their silences usually were. Vivien was quite wrong, he and she were not still in love. It was many years since they had been. But something left over from that time occasionally stirred between them when they were least prepared for it, a memory of pain inflicted on each other, of helplessness and desperation, and self-consciousness would suddenly intrude on their normally affectionate and pleasant relationship.

"I didn't see your car outside," she said. "How did you get here?"

"It bores me, driving out of London," he answered. "I came by train and taxi."

"Have you eaten?" she asked.

"Yes, thanks. When I couldn't get an answer here, I went to the Crown."

"That's where we were ourselves," she said. "It was the Annual Dinner of the Costume Society. We were upstairs."

"So that's what Vivien's doing here," he said. "I suppose she was talking about shoes."

"Yes, she was good too . . ." Christine paused. "What do you mean, when you couldn't get in here?"

"Well, I rang two or three times and nobody answered."

"What time was that?"

"I suppose about eight o'clock."

"And nobody answered?"

"No."

"I don't understand it," she said. "Marsha must have been here."

"The girl who let me in when I came back?"

"Yes."

"What about old Heacham? Why didn't she answer?"

"She'd gone to bed ages earlier and was probably sound asleep. But Marsha should have been here."

She would have thought that Lew and Rodney would have been here too, unless Marsha had managed to get rid of them both with remarkable speed after the rest of the party had left. Had the girl gone out with one or both of them? She was not supposed to go out at night without warning Christine, and not at all if the Findons were going to be out themselves. Theoretically Mrs. Heacham might have counted as a sitter-in for the children, but in fact she slept far too soundly to be left in charge of them.

"Is something wrong?" Simon asked. "You're looking worried."

"A lot of silly little unconnected things seem to have gone wrong today," Christine said. "Lew turning up from nowhere and upsetting his mother by it, and Vivien's shoes disappearing, and David lying about having taken them— because I suppose he must have, I can't think of anyone else who would dream of doing it—and Marsha apparently going out when she's supposed to stay in with the children. And I've always felt I could trust her completely. But perhaps I can't. Perhaps she's getting bored with the job and isn't going to go on being reliable."

"And me turning up too and having to be put to bed on your sofa," Simon said. "I'm sorry about that, Christine. I really wouldn't have come if I'd dreamt how full up you were."

"Why *have* you come, Simon?" she asked. "Is there any special reason. I mean, is anything wrong?"

He sat down beside her, took her hand and rubbed it gently against his cheek. He was often mildly demonstrative to her, as if to convince both of them that there was nothing hurtful left over from the old days.

"Not a thing," he said. "I just suddenly felt fed up with everything, and thought that a day or two with you and Henry was what I needed. You usually help me to sort myself out. But of course I ought to have telephoned first. Only I'm not used to finding your home a whirling maelstrom of humanity."

"Nor am I," she said.

"I'll push off tomorrow."

"No, don't."

"Well, we'll see."

He stood up and wandered off down the room. He looked oddly forlorn, as if for once life were getting the better of him. She had seen these moods in him before and knew that as a rule they did not last long. This one might be over by tomorrow. Probably the trouble was some relationship with a woman which had become too enveloping for him, demanding more of him than he was inclined to give, and because he was not actually hardhearted or insensitive, the problem of extricating himself was causing him sharp, painful spasms of guilt and self-contempt. Simon often did not like himself very much.

Yet, once you knew him well, he was very likeable, as well as good-looking and attractive. In the days when Christine had been in love with him, she had thought that if she could not have him, she would be prepared to spend the rest of her days on a desert island. But then, when they had been so near to deciding to get married that one day he had suggested that she should meet his family, and had taken her to their house in Wimbledon for the day, Henry had been there. And she had afterwards realised that that very unusual thing had happened to her, she had fallen in love at first sight.

Of course, in a sense it had not been love at first sight, because of the similarity between the two brothers. Almost all that had attracted her in Simon was there in Henry, while several of the things that had kept her wary of Simon were not. Her feeling for Simon had begun to feel a merely immature kind of infatuation.

Put like that, it all sounded very simple. Of course, at the time, it had not been simple at all. For two or three months she had gone on believing that she was in love with Simon and had tended to blame him for the feeling that something had gone out of their relationship. In the end it had been Henry who had suddenly taken matters into his own hands, had explained to her the true state of her emotions, had told Simon, and had driven her off with him in a caravan to the Highlands.

It had been nearly two years after that before she had seen Simon again, and for far longer than two years she

had gone on feeling a nagging sense of guilt whenever she
met him, although by then her place had been taken by
enough women for her to be happy to forget that she had
ever thought that she meant anything to him. Henry had
assured her that this sense of guilt was mainly her vanity,
and that the truth of the matter was that she was the one
woman whom Simon had managed to shed without any hurt
to her heart or her pride, and that he was duly grateful, and
she knew that this was likely to be right. But it seemed that
her vanity was very stubborn and demanded to be indulged,
for she had never quite lost the feeling that she owed something to Simon that she could never quite pay off. Henry
said that she did not want to pay it off, and she felt a little
secret pleasure when he said it, because it was about the
only sign of jealousy that he had ever given.

Henry came in and seeing Simon, asked if he was staying
for the weekend, then poured out drinks for the three of
them and they sat round the fire, talking quietly. Like Christine, Henry asked Simon if anything was wrong, and Simon
answered as before that he had merely felt that he would
like a quiet couple of days with the two of them. He had
forgotten that they had David and Frances staying with
them, he said, and until she had let him in at the door, that
they had an *au pair* girl.

"Tell me about her," he said. "Did you advertise that
beauty was your main requirement?"

"We didn't advertise at all," Christine said. "Ena found
her for us. Her father died years ago and her mother got
married again this summer and went to live in South Africa,
and Marsha wouldn't go with her because of apartheid and
so on, so she stayed behind to study Domestic Science at
the college here, and she's turned out a pearl beyond price.
She's not only lovely, she's sweet and kind and obliging
and the children love her. But I'm worried at her not answering the bell when you rang, Simon. She's supposed
to stay here with the children when we go out. Mrs. Heacham goes to bed early, takes a sleeping pill and wouldn't
hear the children screaming if the house was on fire, so
we'd never think of relying on her, and Marsha knows that.

And we don't go out so often that she's any cause for complaint."

"Probably being left here with two competitive young males was a bit much for her and they all went out together," Henry said. "Anyway, everything's all right. I looked in on the children just now and they're sound asleep."

"How are you getting along with old Heacham?" Simon asked.

Henry grinned. "Ask Christine. I don't suffer much myself. Mrs. Heacham belongs to the school that believes a wife should be taught that her husband's the boss of the house. I miss Christine's cooking. Our food used to be a lot more interesting than it is now. But it's Christine who bears the brunt."

"I'm sorry for the old woman," Simon said. "The best time of her life must have been when she was working for Father. I suppose there was a sort of happiness for her in her devotion to him, but all she got back from him was a sort of respectful gratitude. Then the way Louis ran off . . . There's an emptiness in the picture that makes it appallingly bleak."

"If you're so sorry for her," Christine said, "why don't you take her off our hands? She'd devote herself to you with passion, just as she did to your father. It's me about the place that she can't stand. She needs a solitary man to look after."

"Now wait, now wait!" Simon said quickly. "You should know I'm very good at feeling sorry for people without having the slightest intention of doing anything for them. Being solitary in my service flat suits me, and that's how I'm going on. But what are you going to do about her if you're finding her such a trial?"

"I wish I knew," Christine said.

"You could just say you can't afford her," Simon suggested.

"But we pay her hardly anything. She insisted on coming for next to nothing. She said she had the pension your father left her, and her old age pension, and had no use for money. All she wanted was kind, familiar faces round her. And she eats next to nothing. She's got an ulcer. Unluckily that means we all have to live on things like boiled chicken and steamed fish, but even so, she hardly picks at them."

"Then come out into the open and say you're happier alone."

Christine sighed and the sigh turned into a great yawn. She suddenly felt extremely tired.

"It seems so brutal, she hasn't anywhere else to go," she said. "She hasn't any friends or relations and she'd be completely alone. That's what she's scared of."

"She's got Louis, hasn't she?"

That was a new thought. Christine had not yet taken in the fact that Mrs. Heacham had Lew again.

"You mean she might be persuaded that she ought to make a home for him," she said. "That's a beautiful thought, Simon."

"Only it wouldn't work," Henry said. "I doubt if Lew's looking for a home at the moment."

"Then why did he come here?" Simon asked. "If someone turns up out of the blue there's always a reason, even if he keeps it to himself. I know it's a habit I have myself, but you know my reason. I suddenly get the feeling that I'd be the better for a little of your company. What's Louis's reason?"

"Mrs. Heacham says he wants money," Christine said. "She says he came to get it from Henry and me. Lew himself says he simply wanted to let bygones be bygones and to make peace with his mother."

"Which you don't believe?"

"I'm not sure."

"I suppose both could be more or less true at the same time," Simon said. "What's Lew like?"

"Very good-looking," she said, "and marvellous with the children, and he does odd jobs, at which, of course, it's possible to make quite a good living nowadays. I think he's quite a hard worker in his way. He cleaned the car for us this afternoon, and did some gardening."

"Well, he doesn't sound the kind I can offer a job to," Simon said. "I was just wondering . . . Well, those Heachams get one with a sort of sense of obligation, don't they?

Those years she was with Father—it was a long time. And Louis was always around, looking ill-treated, though I don't suppose he actually was, but anyway not getting the kind of chance in life that you and I had, Henry. So one has the feeling that one owes them something. But he doesn't sound like promising material for work in an office."

"Who'd have thought you'd ever be that when you were his age?" Henry said. "I remember you wanted to own an aeroplane and run a charter service. Then you wanted to go exploring in Brazil. Then you wanted to get a job as a foreign correspondent for some newspaper. And you had other projects. I don't remember them all."

Simon grinned. "And then the adventure of getting rich suddenly struck me, didn't it? And it seemed more practical than most of my other ideas, so I got down to that and stuck to it. Has Louis ever had any training of any kind, do you know?"

"It doesn't sound like it," Henry said.

"Suppose I offered to pay for it," Simon said, "how would he respond?"

Simon had never grown tight-fisted with wealth, or afraid that other people wanted to exploit him. He was extremely generous.

"If you mean it, I think you'd better sound him out yourself," Henry answered. "I don't know how long he plans to stay, but he'll certainly be here tomorrow."

"Well, I'll see when I've talked to him. I'd like to help him, if possible."

"But you won't help us with Mrs. Heacham," Christine said.

"Not on your life, my darling."

She gave another yawn, then said that she was going to bed, but that she would fetch Simon some sheets and blankets first, went to get them, then left him and Henry together.

Henry followed her up to bed after ten minutes or so. The rain was beating hard on the windowpanes and the blustery wind had risen. It howled in the chimney of their room with a peculiar eeriness, whining like an imprisoned animal. She had often said that because of the noise it made, they ought to have the chimney blocked off, but they had never got around to doing it. That night, as she sometimes did, she found herself listening to it and unable to sleep. She did not know whether it was the noise that kept her awake and so let her start thinking, or whether it was her thoughts that made her wakeful and so let her notice the noise. Whichever it was, she could not sleep, and long after Henry's breathing had told her that he was asleep, she lay there, listening to those muffled shrieks in the chimney and the battering of rain on the window, and fretting over all sorts of problems that seemed to grow bigger and bigger as the night progressed.

The problem of Vivien's shoes, for instance. Christine had said that they would replace them. But that was liable to cost at least fifty pounds. Probably more. And she had all sorts of other uses for any fifty pounds that they had to spare. But if they could not get David to admit what he had done with the shoes, what could they do but take responsibility?

It was a great pity, she felt, that she had not had more experience with children. With David looking them all in the eye and smiling and telling them a blatant lie, she had not the faintest idea how to deal with him. Ought she to have threatened him? Ought she to have wheedled? Ought she to try to explain to him now about that fifty pounds? To her, as a child, fifty pounds would have sounded an enormous sum and she would have been petrified at the thought that any action of hers could have involved her parents in spending so much. But what with inflation and all, what did fifty pounds mean to a modern child? Of course, Vivien might refuse to be reimbursed. But that would be generosity on her part. They had no right to expect it of her.

Then suppose it was not David who had taken the shoes?

She thought of his smiles, his evasive looks when he was questioned, and his obvious enjoyment of the fact that the shoes had disappeared, and that Vivien, to whom he appeared to have taken an instant dislike, was being seriously inconvenienced. It had to be David who had taken them.

If not, who else could it possibly have been?

In an adult, she thought, it would be the action of a lunatic, and so far as she knew, no one in the household was as far over the edge as that. Some of them might not be as well-balanced as they ought to be. She could act rather oddly herself when she had not been given time to simmer down between bouts, as it were, of contact with other people. But when she was suffering from over-much human companionship, the way that it took her was headaches, attacks of bad temper, flustered forgetfulness and daydreams about beautiful solitary holidays on the shores of the Mediterranean. She had never, to the best of her knowledge, gone creeping into anyone else's bedroom, rifling their suitcases and stealing any of their belongings.

Henry, as a possible culprit, she simply ruled out. She had relied on his sanity to support her own shaky stability for too long ever to consider doing anything to undermine that precious prop.

Then there was Mrs. Heacham. A very neurotic woman. But honest to the bone where material things were concerned. As she had often proclaimed, she would never take a farthing that did not belong to her. And Christine believed her. Yet was she by any chance accepting Mrs. Heacham's honesty a little too easily at its face value? Even if she would never take money, or jewellery, or even a postage stamp, which had an obvious monetary value, might she not, just conceivably, have become sufficiently mentally disturbed recently, without anyone realising it, to help herself to Vivien's shoes? The urge to do it might have come from a female envy of Vivien's elegance, or a general envy strong enough to make her want to spoil her evening for her. Only if it was the second of these, why not simply take the evening shoes? Why take them all?

Then what about Marsha? She had plenty of pretty shoes of her own, gold, silver, scarlet, blue, white, grey, brown, black. And since she had never met Vivien before in her life, it seemed unlikely that she would want to spoil her evening. Such a thing did not fit her nature either. Besides she had an alibi. She had been making the tea, then had been in the sitting room when the shoes must have been stolen.

There remained Lew Heacham. But what could his motive have been? Was he a foot fetishist? What exactly was a foot fetishist? Someone with the odd habit of falling in love with shoes, wasn't it? And sadism and masochism came into it somehow.

Damn psychology! she thought. Most of us nowadays know just enough about it to entertain the most ridiculous-sounding ideas about things, without knowing enough to make any guess as to whether or not the ideas just might be true. Could one tell a foot fetishist by looking at him? Lew Heacham looked normal enough. And the way that he had looked at Marsha had seemed normal enough, too. But perhaps he had only been thinking about her feet, and wanting her to kick him or do something equally odd.

Christine supposed that she ought not to leave Vivien herself out of her list of suspects. Only she could not think of any conceivable reason why she should have stolen her own shoes, or hidden them, rather, or simply left them at home, or perhaps merely kept them in her suitcase and said that they were missing. She had accepted Lew's suggestion of the bandage and the bedroom slipper with enthusiasm, so hiding the shoes could not have been a complicated way of getting out of going to the dinner and giving her talk, and what other reason could she have had for such an odd masquerade? No, Vivien didn't fit the bill.

It had to be David.

At last Christine fell asleep. But it was fitful sleep, and by seven o'clock she was wide awake, once more, again going over her arguments of the night before. About eight o'clock she got up. She put on slacks and a sweater, went downstairs, took the chain off the front door, took in the milk and the Sunday paper, went to the kitchen and made herself some tea. As it was Sunday, no one else would think of appearing before nine o'clock at the earliest. The house seemed wonderfully peaceful. The wind had dropped and no busy traffic sounds came from the street. The morning was as quiet as it would have been deep in the country.

But she still could not stop thinking about those shoes. If David had taken them, what, she asked herself, had he done with them? He had not had long to dispose of them. He had only had the time after Vivien had left her room to come downstairs for tea and before Lew had gone up to the children's room, where Christine had found him helping Frances with the jigsaw puzzle. How long had that been? Ten minutes? Something like that. And David would have been in a hurry anyway, because he could not have known how soon someone would notice that something was amiss. His instinct would have been to grab the shoes and somehow get rid of them immediately. So there was no need to think of complicated hiding places.

In his place, what would Christine herself have done?

Marsha and she had already looked in all the more obvious places in the house. But what about the garden? It had not occurred to either of them to look outside. Suppose he had simply raced downstairs with his stolen goods in his arms, let himself out by the back door, which he could have reached without going through the kitchen, where he might have encountered Mrs. Heacham, hurled the shoes out into the darkness and fled upstairs again?

No, it would not have been dark yet . . .

But perhaps she was thinking along the right lines. He might have dashed out to the garage and dumped the shoes there in a corner, or even in the boot of the car.

Christine finished her tea quickly, unlocked the back door and let herself out into the garden.

She searched the garage thoroughly. It did not take long. There were not many places where anything could be hidden. The shoes were not there. But she noticed something unexpected while she was looking round. The car, which had looked so fine and shiny after Lew had cleaned it, was rain-spotted and splashed with mud. So someone had had it out last night, after the rain had begun.

Marsha, of course. She had been given a spare key so that she could take the children out. So she had definitely been out last night at the time when Simon had first called at the house. It was very annoying. Christine was going to have to speak severely to her about her responsibilities. And she was not accustomed to speaking severely to people. When she had done it, she would probably feel as guilty as if she had tried to pick an unjustified quarrel with the girl. Unhappily, she strolled back towards the back door.

Suddenly she stood still. She was almost at the door and she was looking down the garden. There at the bottom of it were the black remains of Lew's bonfire, and as she looked at it, an extremely unpleasant idea had come into her mind. Such an obvious idea, once she had thought of it, that it sent her running across the wet lawn to where the ashes of the bonfire that had not been blown away by last night's gale clung together in a sodden heap on the paved path. And she was right, the shoes were there, all four of them.

She knelt down and started drawing them carefully out of the ashes, the half-burned dead leaves and charred twigs that were matted round them. The shoes must have been thrust into the heart of the fire while it was still burning quite strongly. There was nothing left of the bedroom slipper but a heel and a soft grey feathery mass that fell apart when she touched it. The gold sandal had not been burned quite away but was completely blackened, with its thin sole curled up and split. The other two shoes, the walking shoe and the shoe of black patent leather, had not lost their shapes, but were damaged beyond redemption.

"Oh, David, David," she muttered looking at the ruins, "you horrid, horrid little boy!"

As she said it a sound reached her from the house that made her sit back on her heels with a jerk and drop the shoes that she was holding. The sound was not unlike the screeching of the wind in the chimney that she had listened to for most of the night, but was weirder and wilder because it was human. She had no doubt at all that it was human. Someone in the house was screaming her head off. A moment later the back door, which she had left half-closed, was flung wide open and Linda Deeping came racing across the lawn towards her.

"Oh, Mrs. Findon!" she wailed. "Mrs. Findon!"

Her pink hair was like a flickering flame nibbling at the edges of her paper-white face. She was wearing black jeans and a thigh-length nylon overall.

Christine had just time to get to her feet, wondering what Linda was doing here on a Sunday, though, as she had a key of her own, she did not wonder about how she had got

in, when she clutched Christine by the arm and screamed
her own name right into her ear, "Mrs. Findon!"

"Yes," Christine said. "Yes—what is it?"

"Oh, it's so awful!" Linda cried. "It's so horrible. I got
the blood on my hand—look!" It was true, there was a dull
smear that looked like dried blood on her long, thin fingers.
"I nearly died. I can't stand blood."

"I don't like it much myself," Christine said, reacting to
Linda's hysteria as she usually did to anyone else's intense
excitement by becoming outwardly unnaturally calm. Inside, her heart was racing. "What is it, Linda?"

"Joe'll tell you. Joe—!" She went running back towards
the house as Police Constable Deeping appeared at the back
door, wearing a painter's overall. He had evidently arrived
that morning to paint the storeroom. His wife flung herself
upon him and hid her face on his breast.

He looked at Christine over Linda's pink head.

"I'm sorry, Mrs. Findon. It's Mrs. Heacham in one of
the trunks." His air, as he announced that he had just found
a corpse in the storeroom, was one of embarrassed apology.
"I was moving it to set the stepladder up by the window,
and Linda was helping me, and we saw she'd got this blood
on her hand. It had rubbed off the handle of the trunk. Then
I saw there were a few spots on the floor too, so I opened
the trunk . . ." He gave a slight cough, as if he were confessing to having taken a liberty. "There's a hammer inside
with her. Someone hit her over the head with it, perhaps
didn't mean to kill her, I don't know, but she's dead. Now,
if you don't mind, I'll use your telephone and tell them
about it at the police station."

# 5

Police Constable Deeping turned to go to the telephone. Over his shoulder, he added, "You won't go into the store-room, will you, Mrs. Findon? No one ought to go in till Superintendent Ditteridge gets here."

She thought how convenient it was to have the corpses in your house discovered by the police themselves. It meant that you knew, right from the start, what you were supposed to do about it. If she had not been told not to go into the storeroom, she might easily have felt that it was actually her duty to go in and make quite sure that Mrs. Heacham was dead and that there was nothing that anyone could do for her.

"Her son's here in the house," she said. "Oughtn't I to tell him what's happened?"

"I can't see any harm in it," Joe Deeping said. "He's got to know sometime, like everyone else in the house. Just as well to tell them, perhaps, before our chaps start streaming in. Just so long as no one goes into the storeroom."

"Yes, all right." She followed him as far as the kitchen as he went to the telephone in Henry's study.

She would have run upstairs then to shake Henry awake and tell him what had happened, and then gone to find Lew, but Linda Deeping's screams had already roused most of the household. Christine had only reached the kitchen door when Lew Heacham came leaping down the stairs and

nearly knocked her over as she tried to get in his way in
case he should rush straight into the storeroom. He clutched
her to stop her falling, and she clutched him to prevent him
going on. They were almost in an embrace.

"Don't, Lew—wait!" she said. "No one's to go in there.
It's terrible, but—but it'll be best to wait."

"It's Mum, isn't it?" he said. His eyes had a shocked,
scared look. "What's she doing? What set her off?"

"What's she—?" Christine realised suddenly that he
thought that it was his mother who had been screaming.
She gave him an uneasy pat on the shoulder. "Come and
sit down, Lew," she said. "I was just coming to look for
you. It's your mother, but—well, it was Mrs. Deeping
screaming. She found your mother, Lew. Something happened to her. She's—well, she's dead."

It was not a brilliant effort. She felt very ashamed of it
as she blundered from one sentence to the next and tried
to draw Lew into the kitchen to sit down. Then, of course,
she meant to offer him tea, or brandy, or whatever else he
wanted. But she could not get him to a chair. He looked
at her blindly with a queer squinting gaze, then shouldered
her out of his way and made straight for the storeroom.

She called after him to stop and Linda Deeping tried to
get in his way, but he knocked her aside and went in.

They heard him give a short, hoarse cry, then there was
silence in the storeroom.

A moment later he came out. He was swaying a little as
he walked and he was squinting worse than ever, like a
drunken man who cannot focus his eyes. He grabbed the
back of a chair, slumped down on it, folded his arms on
the table and dropped his face onto them.

Christine and Linda stood there, saying nothing. Then
Joe Deeping returned, arriving together with Henry. Joe
had apparently told Henry what had happened, for he did
not try to go to the storeroom or ask any questions, but put
an arm round Christine's shoulders and drew her close to
his side. It was comforting and steadied her nerves.

Linda said, "He went in to look at her, Joe. Mrs. Findon
and me tried to stop him, but we couldn't hold him."

Lew lifted his head. There were no tears in his eyes but

his mouth was trembling. "Wouldn't you have done it too if she'd been your mother? Your mother whom you haven't seen for six years. You come home to make your peace with her, and the very next day somebody murders her, with her still believing you only came to her just for money." He looked at Joe Deeping. "It *was* last night it happened, wasn't it, not this morning? I mean, the blood's dry."

"It looks like that," Joe answered gruffly. "But I'm no expert."

While Lew had been speaking both Marsha and Vivien had appeared in the kitchen doorway. Both were in slacks and sweater, but Marsha's hair was dishevelled, whereas Vivien's was as well-groomed as always.

"What's happened, Henry?" she asked. "I was woken by some hideous screams. It's a most unpleasant experience, being woken by screams. I thought I was in the middle of a nightmare."

"So you are, in a fashion," Henry answered. "Mr. and Mrs. Deeping came here this morning to paint the store-room, and they found Mrs. Heacham's body in one of the trunks in there. I gather her head's almost split open, and it can't be anything but murder."

Vivien blinked her eyes several times, but otherwise showed very little reaction. Marsha's face blanched and she looked as if she were going to be sick. But just then there were light footsteps behind her and David and Frances, both in pyjamas and dressing gowns, tried to get past her and Vivien into the kitchen.

"What's happening?" David demanded. "What were the noises? What's everyone doing here? What's the matter with Lew?"

Marsha showed her quality quickly. She grabbed each child by an arm, spun them round, and saying, "Why aren't you dressed? You won't get any breakfast till you're dressed. Come on, we're going upstairs," she hauled them away with her to the stairs. They protested and went on asking questions, but she kept them going, talking them down as if she did not hear what they were saying.

"Murder," Lew muttered, as if talking to himself. "Her head split open. Blood. So life goes on."

Henry stood looking down at him thoughtfully.

"Lew, why did you really come here?" he asked.

"I've told you," Lew said, "it was to make peace. It was—just to see her again. But she didn't believe that herself, so who else is going to?"

"Why shouldn't we believe you?"

"Because you don't understand." Lew rested his head on his hand. His voice was flat and weary. "You don't understand what it's like to feel that you haven't got a single person who cares about you, and that you've brought that on yourself, because the only person who ever did care— well, in a way you hated her, because she was so hard with you and always seemed to stand between you and everything you wanted. So you deliberately hurt her as badly as you knew how. You didn't understand then that when she was hard with you it was out of love, needing you so badly because she'd got nothing herself—just other people's homes, and other people's tolerance. Their chilly tolerance. Because that's all you ever gave her, isn't it? None of you cared for her. You only put up with her because you see yourselves as such nice, generous, kindhearted people. The same with me when I turned up—poor Lew who'd had such a dim sort of childhood. But how lucky for us now he's here to be a scapegoat, since we've got this nasty murder in our midst."

"I shouldn't say that sort of thing if I were you, Lew," Simon said. He had just appeared in the kitchen in a dressing gown. "I think I'd keep quite quiet."

"That's what I was going to say," Joe Deeping said. "I'd save it all for when Superintendent Ditteridge gets here. It won't be long now."

It was, in fact, only three or four minutes. Christine had made more tea, put cups and saucers and a loaf of bread and some butter and marmalade on the table, so that people could help themselves to some breakfast or not, as they wanted, when the front doorbell rang and Henry went to answer it.

The Superintendent came in with three other men, one in plain clothes, like himself, and two in uniform. Christine had heard of him so often from Linda Deeping, usually in connection with his ferocious little cairn bitch, Pippy, that she somehow half-expected to see Pippy cradled in his arms. She also expected him to be a somewhat forbidding figure, stern and self-important. In fact, he looked a quiet sort of man with a remote, almost uninterested way of looking at people, as if the human face were something that filled him with a marked lack of enthusiasm. But he seemed to try to mask this with an air of good-natured courtesy. He was an ageing man, tall, with close-cropped, bristly grey hair and restless, light brown eyes.

He told them, please, to go on with their breakfast, while he and his colleagues went into the storeroom. They were in there for some time. Then one of them took charge of the telephone in Henry's study and began a series of calls. These in due course brought a doctor to the house, an ambulance, men with cameras, with fingerprinting apparatus and all the other paraphernalia of a murder inquiry. But before they had arrived Mr. Ditteridge had taken over the study, saying that he would appreciate it if he could speak to all the members of the household one by one, and since Mr. Findon was the householder, could he begin with him?

Henry was following the Superintendent into the study when he paused. "Superintendent, my brother arrived here last night to stay for the weekend. Mrs. Richmond and my wife and I had gone out to a dinner, but Miss Lindale should have been here. Yet when he rang, he got no answer. So it looks as if the house may have been empty for a certain time except for the children and Mrs. Heacham herself. So someone could perhaps have got in then from outside."

"Has there been a burglary?" Simon asked, then with swift anxiety, "Not the snuffboxes!"

The snuffboxes had not even entered Christine's mind until that moment, and she was sure had not been in Henry's either, but as soon as Simon said that, they both thrust past Mr. Ditteridge to a corner of the study and looked anxiously into the cabinet that hung on the wall there.

The collection of snuffboxes in the cabinet was part of what the Findons had inherited from Henry's father at the same time as the legacy with which they had bought their house. As a collection, so they had always understood, it was not outstanding. He had never specialized in any period, or type, but had bought the boxes as they happened to take his fancy, whether of wood, horn, papier-mâché, ivory, silver, or gold. Nevertheless, the contents of that corner cabinet were probably worth more than the rest of the contents of the house put together.

"No, not been touched," Henry said. "Everything's there. So it looks as if robbery wasn't the motive."

"Poor old Heacham," Simon muttered. "I suppose she was poking her nose in as usual where she wasn't wanted."

"But it could have been robbery, couldn't it, even if the snuffboxes weren't taken?" Christine said. "We haven't had time to see if anything else is gone."

"That's true, Mrs. Findon," Mr. Ditteridge said. "If you could take a look, see if anything's gone from anyone's handbag, any jewellery missing, and so on, that would be useful."

She nodded and went out, followed by Simon.

"I think I'll get dressed," he said. "A dressing gown feels a little informal for a murder. Christine—"

"Yes?"

"Do you think Henry's right about when it happened?"

"They haven't said anything about that yet," she answered, "but it does seem likely, doesn't it?"

"When I came and rang the bell and nobody seemed to hear. Why *didn't* they hear, Christine?"

"I don't know. We'll have to ask Marsha."

"If it was then, the children may have been all alone in the house with the murderer?"

"That's how it looks."

"I wonder if they heard anything."

"I'm going to talk to them now," she said. "I'll ask them."

"Aren't you going to check up on the money and jewellery, as the policeman asked you?"

"Yes, but I think I'll talk to the children first. If they realise they were probably alone with the murderer, it's the sort of thought that might give birth to nightmares and David's rather prone to them already. He's got altogether too much imagination for his own good."

"Christine—"

"Yes?"

"The number of times I've said someone ought to murder that old woman . . ."

"Don't!" she said. "I know."

"She was terribly unloved, wasn't she? Not hated, just not loved. But being unloved doesn't usually get you murdered. So I suppose it was your prowler, not an inside job."

"An *inside* job!" Christine exclaimed. "One of *us*, do you mean?"

"Well, there are odd undercurrents in your home just now, do you know that? Perhaps you're too used to them to notice it. But everything, even last night, felt slightly abnormal."

"Everything last night was *very* abnormal," she said. "That business of Vivien's shoes . . . But it wasn't what I'd call murderously abnormal."

Simon smiled. "Anyway, I'm not going to find the peace and quiet I came for, am I? Now I'll go and shave."

He went upstairs to the bathroom. Christine went to the children's room.

She found David and Frances sitting very close together on the window seat in their room, both looking subdued and scared. Marsha was standing by the fireplace, where she had lit the gas fire, and seemed to be trying to warm some bitter chill out of her blood.

"So you told them," Christine said.

"No, I didn't," Marsha said quickly. "I didn't know what you'd want me to do, so I—I waited for you."

"What's upset them then?"

"It's the police," Marsha said. "They don't understand."

David flung up his head and looked Christine fiercely in the face. "I didn't do it!" he declared in ringing tones. "I swear I didn't. You didn't have to send for the police."

She felt stunned. "But no one thinks—how could they?— my dears, nobody's thought for a moment . . ."

"But don't you see," Marsha said in her gentle voice, "it's the shoes they're thinking about? They don't know anything about—the other."

"And I didn't take them!" David cried. "I never even

thought of it. I never went into her room. I'm not a thief.
You didn't have to send for the police."

"He didn't take them," Frances echoed him. "He'd have
told if he had, and he didn't. We only wished we *had* taken
them. She was so silly about it, that Mrs. Richmond, that
we wished we'd thought of it. It would have served her
right for being so silly. But we don't know anything about
it."

"I'm afraid there's been a mix-up," Christine said. "The
police aren't here because of the shoes—"

"I didn't take them!" David interrupted, standing up and
facing her as if she were his worst enemy. "But when I
heard about it I wished, I wished I'd thought of it. I wanted
you to think I had. So I sort of said I hadn't taken them as
if perhaps I had. But I didn't say I had. I didn't tell any
lies. I didn't *actually* pretend I'd taken them."

So that was the explanation of his slyness the evening
before. He had not admitted taking the shoes, he had merely
managed to look guilty because he would so much have
liked to have had the brilliant idea of stealing them. A subtle
little piece of acting. Not that that seemed important at the
moment.

"They haven't had any breakfast," Marsha said. "Shall
I go and get something on a tray?"

"Yes, will you?" Christine said. "And for yourself too.
And I'll try to explain . . ."

She did not look forward to it. How much ought she to
tell? She had not the faintest idea what children of their
ages could take in, how much or how little they really
needed to know. Drawing a chair towards them, she sat
down and tried to think of how to begin.

Frances immediately got up and came to her, climbed
onto her knee and put her arms round her neck.

"When I grow up I want to be a policeman," she said.

"Stupid!" David said. "You'd have to be a policewoman."

"I want to be a police sergeant and ride on a big horse,"
she said.

"They don't have policewomen riding on horses," David
said.

"I could be the first one then," she said in her sensible way.

"Listen," Christine said. "Do, please, listen just for a moment. I said the police aren't here because of the shoes. But something else happened last night . . . I'm afraid you'll be very sorry when you hear it, but Mrs. Heacham died last night. We found her this morning in the storeroom. So that's why we sent for the police. There's no need for you to be frightened."

They both became silent and thoughtful and Frances got off Christine's knee and went to sit beside David again, pressing his side, as if that gave her more feeling of security, when faced with the facts of life and death, than Christine could give her.

After a moment David asked, "Do you always have to send for the police when people die?"

"Sometimes," Christine said.

"We didn't when Granny died, we just had the doctor."

"The doctor's here too."

"Why was she in the storeroom?" Frances asked. "It's a funny place for her to be."

"It is, rather."

"What was she doing there?"

"We don't know."

"I suppose she was murdered," David said calmly. "She heard a noise down there and she went down to investigate and surprised an intruder."

Frances at once began to cry. "I don't want to be murdered!" she wailed. "I want to go away! I want Mummy!"

Oh God, Christine thought, television, newspapers, detective stories!

"Shut up!" David said irritably. "Mummy's in America. And nobody's going to murder you. It was Mrs. Heacham they came to get because she knew too much."

"I thought you said it was because she heard a noise," Frances said. "*I* heard a noise, but I didn't get up. I'm glad I didn't get up."

"You didn't hear anything," David said. "You're just making it up."

"I did," she said. "You aren't the only person who doesn't tell lies. I did hear a noise."

"What kind of noise?" Christine asked more excitedly than she meant to.

"Oh, just a noise," Frances said. "Sort of like a bell ringing and a door shutting."

"You heard the doorbell?" Christine thought of Simon arriving and ringing and getting no answer. "And then you heard the door shut?" That did not fit. "How long after?"

"I'm not sure it was after, perhaps it was before," she said.

"You're just dreaming," David said. "People open and shut doors *after* the bell rings, not before it."

"Perhaps it was after," she agreed.

Christine decided that her interrogation would not get her very far and dropped it. But at least the children seemed to have taken the fact of a murder having happened in the house pretty well in their stride, for which she was thankful. She waited until she heard footsteps outside on the landing, then went to the door and opened it for Marsha to come in with the tray.

She was followed in by Simon.

"All right if I join you?" he asked. "The kitchen's been occupied by foreign troops."

There was milk for the children on the tray, a pot of tea and cups, a packet of Ryvita, and a butterdish. Marsha put the tray down on the table, leaving it to Christine to pour out the tea, and backed once more towards the gas fire, standing still in front of it, looking somehow both crushed and determined. She seemed smaller than usual and more fragile, while the delicate bones of her face seemed more defined, more mature. She had brushed her thick fair hair since leaving the room, and as she faced Christine, she put up both her hands and pulled it back from her face, as if she wanted to strip herself of a disguise.

"There's something I've got to tell you," she said abruptly. "I went out last night."

"I know," Christine said.

"You know—? Has Lew told you?"

"No, but I've been out in the garage and it was obvious

the car had been taken out after the rain started. And when Simon first came here and rang the bell, there seems to have been no one here to answer it."

"Oh . . ." Marsha let her hair fall loose again and her hands drop to her sides. "I know I oughtn't to have gone. It was completely irresponsible. And I want to say I'm sorry."

"What made you do it?" Christine asked, as she poured out the milk for David and Frances, then started to fill the teacups on the tray.

"It's just that Roddie was so impossible," Marsha said. "He wouldn't settle down and be friendly, and he wouldn't go away either. He just stood and glowered at Lew, because he—oh, just because he was there. It wasn't Lew's fault. He hadn't done anything to provoke it."

Simon gave a laugh and said, "But he was there, as you said, and that's sometimes a pretty powerful reason for hating a person. I'm on Roddie's side at the moment." He looked at Christine. "Is that Rodney Maskell, the son of those friends of yours? How the young do grow up!"

The pink in Marsha's cheeks deepened a little. "He was just being a nuisance. And that began to amuse Lew and he started to tease him. And I didn't like that, so I said what a pity it was that it had started to rain, because Roddie would get so wet walking home, so suppose I drove him. I was thinking, you see, Lew would be here, so it wouldn't matter if I was gone for a little while."

"But that was too much for Lew," Simon said. "He didn't like being left behind. And Roddie didn't like being turned out, even with such delicate tact. So then things began to get quite unpleasant, and it upset you that you couldn't control them, so you said they could both come—thinking, of course, it would only be a few minutes and it wouldn't matter anyway."

She turned on him with her blue eyes glittering. "Well, what would you have done?"

"Just what you did, I'm sure," he said. "Young men can be perfectly intolerable. It's often necessary to take a strong line."

Her glare became uncertain. "But I oughtn't to have . . ."

She turned back to Christine. "You see, it wasn't just that. If we'd just dumped Roddie and come back, it wouldn't have been quite so bad. But on the way back, when we were passing the Black Bull, we thought we'd stop for a quick drink. So we did, and altogether we were out for about half an hour, I suppose. And that's when—isn't it?— *he* got in? And we could easily have had the drink at home, so—so there's no excuse for me."

"I suppose Lew was driving," Simon said.

"He was, as a matter of fact," Marsha admitted.

"And when you got to the Bull, he just stopped the car and said, 'Come on, we're going in for a drink.'"

"Well, more or less."

Simon turned to Christine with a pleased smile. "You see how nice she is, Christine. She wasn't going to put the blame on Lew, when it was obviously all his fault. And the kids were all right, so there's no reason to worry."

"Except that that's when *he* got in!" Marsha insisted, with a sound of tears in her voice. It was as if she could have stood up to an attack from Christine, but this unsolicited support was too much for her. "If I'd been here, he might never have got in."

"On the other hand," Simon said, "we might have found two corpses instead of one."

"Oh . . .!" She gave a swift, apprehensive glance at the two children.

"It's all right," David reassured her composedly, "we know all about it."

Simon nodded. "I was assuming that two reasonably intelligent children would have all the relevant facts at their disposal by now."

Frances suddenly started to bounce up and down on her seat, smiling round at them all delightedly. "Do you know what Mr. Ditteridge will do when he's caught the murderer?" she exclaimed with enthusiasm. "He'll cut him up into little pieces and feed him to Pippy."

They were all silent, digesting this rather startling view of the police, when the door opened and Henry, putting his head in, said that Mr. Ditteridge would like to see Christine.

# 6

Christine remembered, before she went down, that she was supposed to have checked up on whether or not any money or jewellery had been stolen.

She knew that no money could have been taken, for the simple reason that Henry and she never kept more than a few pounds at a time in the house. She had accounts in nearly all the shops to which she went regularly, and if for some reason she happened to be caught short when the bank was closed, the grocer would always cash a cheque. What money she and Henry had about them was usually divided between his wallet and her handbag, and the night before all that had been left of the money that she had cashed on Friday had been in the pocket of Henry's dinner jacket or the note-case in her evening bag. So there had been none lying about for a thief to pick up.

She was not as sure about the jewellery situation. Going to the bedroom, she looked in the leather case where she kept what she had. Nothing had been touched. Garnets, opals, amethysts, and her one and only good diamond ring were all there. Their prowler had not been interested in them.

She told Mr. Ditteridge this when she entered the study.

"But I suppose," he said as she sat down, "you don't know how much money Mrs. Heacham herself may have had on the premises."

"No, but I don't think it would have been much," Christine answered. "She was very nervous of burglars and she had an account at Barclay's Bank in the High Street."

"Do you know if she'd made a will?"

"She said once she had. She told me she was leaving everything she had to some charity or other, as her family hadn't deserved anything of her."

"So her son wouldn't have benefited."

"I suppose not."

"What can you tell me about him?" he asked. "What sort of terms were they on?"

"To the best of my knowledge, she hadn't even heard of him for five years," Christine said, "and she didn't seem particularly glad to see him."

He nodded. "I see. Yet I'm not altogether easy in my mind about that young man. I've got a feeling . . . Still, better not to say anything about that till we've checked."

He had, however, Christine suddenly felt sure, said those few words deliberately, to see if there was any reaction from her.

When she was silent, he went on, "About Mrs. Heacham's movements last night, Mrs. Findon, can you account for her being in the storeroom?"

"Not really," she said, "unless she heard something in there when she brought her tray down."

"Her tray?"

"Yes, she generally had her supper on a tray up in her room. Her health wasn't good—she had an ulcer—and she liked to have just milk and an egg for supper, and she used to like to watch television while she had it. So she used to leave our dinner more or less ready for us, so that Miss Lindale or I just had to add the finishing touches, and she'd take her tray upstairs. Then when she got to a programme that bored her, she'd bring the tray down and pop the things in the dishwasher, and then go up to bed."

"And that would be about when?" he asked.

"It varied," Christine said, "according to the programmes, but I think she was generally in bed by about nine o'clock."

"So she might have come down and heard something in the storeroom, say, about eight to eight-thirty?"

"That's just guessing," Christine said. "Last night she might have done something unusual. She was upset by her son turning up. She went to bed rather earlier than usual, I know that, because I went out to the kitchen a little before six o'clock and she'd gone up already. She'd locked up everywhere, as she always did before she went to bed, and gone."

"You're sure of the time?"

"Pretty sure. We were expecting our friends, Mr. and Mrs. Maskell, for drinks at six, and I'd changed and was ready by that time, and I just popped out to the kitchen to tell Mrs. Heacham that if she'd like her son to stay on for a time it was all right with us, but she'd gone up already. Then I went to the sitting room and I'd been there I suppose ten minutes when the Maskells arrived."

"You say Mrs. Heacham always locked up," Mr. Ditteridge said. "Can you tell me just what she did?"

"She went round all the ground-floor rooms, making sure the window catches were fastened, and she locked and bolted the back door and she put the chain on the front door—she'd do that sometimes even if she knew we were going out, or were expecting friends, as we were last night, or . . ." She stopped.

"Yes?" Mr. Ditteridge said when he had given her a moment to think.

"I'm not sure. It's just that . . ." She felt muddled and looked at him helplessly as if he could sort out the muddle for her. "I'm *not* sure, but I think, when I went into the garden this morning, the back door was locked and bolted, just as usual."

"If it was, then the prowler, if it was a prowler, must have left by the front door, mustn't he?" said Mr. Ditteridge.

"Yes, of course," she said.

"When did she do this locking up, before she took her supper upstairs or after she came down?"

"Oh, before, as soon as it got dark. As I said, she was very nervous of burglars."

"What time did you go into the garden?"

"A bit after eight o'clock, I think."

"For any particular reason, or did you usually do that?"

"No, I... As a matter of fact, I was looking for something. A rather absurd thing happened yesterday afternoon, and I had an idea... But it can't have anything to do with all this, even though I was actually right."

"What was this absurd thing?" he asked in his calm, persistent way.

She told him about the theft of Vivien's shoes and of everyone's suspicions of David, and of how she had found the shoes in the garden in the ashes of the bonfire.

"And Mrs. Richmond missed them when?" he asked.

"I think she actually missed them about six o'clock," Christine said, "when she'd changed and was just going to slip them on and come downstairs to join us and the Maskells in the sitting room. But the shoes must have been taken some time earlier, when we were having tea, because she'd been lying down in her room for about an hour before she changed, and they'd have had to be taken before that. Say between four and half-past."

"And Mrs. Heacham wouldn't have gone upstairs by then, I suppose."

"Oh no, she'd have been having her own tea in the kitchen. I think she and her son had it together." She frowned. "But there can't be any connection between the two things, can there?"

"Not that I can see at present," he answered, "but I'm trying to get a picture in my mind of what everyone was doing and where they were all yesterday evening. We don't know for certain yet, of course, but the doctor thinks Mrs. Heacham was killed between around five-thirty and eight-thirty. You understand, that's only a very rough estimate. He may be able to tell us a bit more after the post-mortem. Not necessarily, though. We generally have to rely on other evidence to tell us when a thing happened."

"How did it happen?" Christine asked. "Mr. Deeping said something about a hammer being left in the trunk."

"That's right. A hammer Mr. Findon says came from your tool rack on the wall of the storeroom. We don't know yet if it was one or more blows on the head that killed her. Her scalp was badly split. That's where the drops of blood came from. We think it happened just inside the door. Then he picked her up and put her in the trunk. Now, Mrs. Findon, can you suggest anything at all to help us? You've told us about the shoes, but can you tell me anything about any other thing that happened yesterday that was, well, call it at all strange?"

Christine sighed and said, "I suppose I ought to tell you about Miss Lindale going out with Rodney Maskell and Lew Heacham, and leaving no one in the house but Mrs. Heacham and the children."

"Ah," he said, and then, as he had already asked so often, "When was that?"

She told him about Marsha's confession. But she suggested that he should get the full story from the girl herself. He agreed, and thanked her for what she had told him, and said that he thought that was all for now.

She went to the sitting room. She found Vivien there, wandering up and down, looking bored and restless. The sheets and blankets that Simon had slept in on the sofa were still there in a rumpled heap. Christine began to fold them up.

"Christine, I've just telephoned Barry," Vivien said. "I said I didn't know when I'd be back, because I suppose the police won't want any of us to leave just at the moment. So he's coming down. He'll probably be here by lunchtime. He's coming by car. You don't mind, do you?... Oh, don't worry, I don't mean he's coming to *stay*. He'll get a room in the Crown or somewhere, and I'll move in with him. Then I shan't be getting under your feet all the time."

"The Crown was full up last night," Christine said. But if there were a room free today, she thought, and Vivien moved into it with Barry, then Simon could be put into the room that she was occupying at present. "Perhaps you ought to ring up and find out if there's a room going today. Of course, there are one or two other hotels in Helsington, but it's the only tolerable one. The number's there on that pad."

Vivien picked up the telephone, dialled, and a moment later told Christine that the Crown had a room free for that night. She went on, "Do you know, Christine, I'm not sure that I'm human," she said. "I'm shocked at what happened to that poor woman, of course, and I'm sorry it's all so upsetting for you and Henry, but what I mainly feel is how nice it would be to be at home and not bothered with it all. Is that very awful?"

"I suppose we all feel a bit of the same thing," Christine said. "We're none of us really grieving for her, unless Lew is, and I'm doubtful about him."

"My guess is that he killed her," Vivien said, "or are there any signs that someone broke in?"

"I don't know. Nothing seems to have been stolen—except, of course, your shoes."

"Oh, damn my shoes!" Vivien said irritably. "That boy took them, that's obvious, but he didn't kill Mrs. Heacham. Anyway, Barry's bringing me some others."

She reached for the telephone again, got through to the Crown, and found that she could book a room for herself and Barry.

"I haven't told you, have I," Christine said as she finished, "I found them—the shoes? On the bonfire that Lew made yesterday afternoon. I'm afraid they're completely ruined, so if you'll let us replace them—"

"Oh, forget them!" Vivien exclaimed. "It wasn't your fault. When Barry gets here we'll move off to the Crown straightaway and have lunch there. You won't want to have to feed extra people here today."

"But about the shoes," Christine said stubbornly, "I'm really not completely convinced that David took them, Vivien. He still says he didn't, and I haven't known him to tell lies before. He says that when he heard about it he wished that he *had* taken them and so he deliberately looked guilty, but that's all he'll admit."

"Then the girl took them," Vivien answered indifferently, "and he's covering up for her. What's the odds? In the bonfire, you said? It's obviously the children. If the things are ruined, as you say, for God's sake, let's forget about them!"

Christine was only too ready to go along with her, having done her best, as she saw it, to do justice to David. But just then Simon came into the room, and he had heard what Vivien had said.

"I've got a theory about those shoes," he said, "and incidentally it's about the murder too, or it just could be."

Vivien threw herself down in a chair.

"Oh God, those shoes!" she said. "It's my own fault, I suppose. I shouldn't have made such a fuss about them last night. But I'd have thought today you'd all be feeling they're pretty unimportant. But go on, Simon. I suppose I'll have to listen."

"Yes, if you don't mind," he said. "This may be quite important. I mean to put it to the police, anyway. My theory is, Vivien, that the wrong shoes were taken. Someone came to the house to steal those antique shoes of yours, and went off with your own by mistake."

"Of all the bird-brained ideas . . . !" Then she paused and looked at him curiously. "What do you mean exactly?"

"I was thinking," Simon said, "if someone wanted those antique shoes, and they knew you'd be here with them, and they sent someone to get them, someone who didn't know anything about such things, but only that he was to get a collection of shoes from your room, and he got into the house and stole the wrong shoes from the suitcase . . ."

"Yes, and then?" she asked with a mocking little smile as he paused.

"Then," he said, "I think the character who'd got the shoes took them out to someone who was waiting somewhere nearby, and was told in simple terms what a fool he'd made of himself, and to go back and get the right ones. So he went back—"

"Dumping Vivien's shoes on the bonfire on the way," Christine interrupted.

"Oh?" Simon had not yet heard about this, so she told him. He nodded and went on, "Yes, dumping them there, as you say, then went back to the back door and probably tried to get up to Vivien's room again. Only by then she was in it, so he hid in the storeroom, waiting for you all to go out, thinking he could try again. But he made some sort of noise in there, and Mrs. Heacham, going her rounds, locking up, found him there and began to scream, so he silenced her . . . No," he said, looking from one of them to the other, "I see you don't believe me."

"There happens to be one very big thing wrong with your theory, Simon," Vivien said. "Aside from questions of time and so on, which I haven't worked out, I can tell you this, that collection of old shoes isn't worth stealing. Shoes don't fetch a great deal on any market. There's a green damask shoe I showed them at the dinner, which is probably the best thing in the collection, and it cost, with its pair, only forty-five pounds. Without its pair, it's worth very little. I doubt if all the shoes I've got here together would fetch a hundred pounds. So a complicated burglary, leading up to murder, just to get hold of them, doesn't seem very likely, does it?"

"But suppose it's someone with an unnatural love for shoes," Simon said. "A foot fetishist."

"Just exactly what *is* a foot fetishist?" Christine asked, remembering how that same idea had come to her in the early hours of the morning.

"Well, there are several sides to it," Vivien said. "In the first place, the foot is a fertility symbol, because it's in constant contact with the earth. Then it's also a symbol of power and the law. The victor used to place his foot on the neck of the vanquished, and kissing a person's foot is a sign of submission and humiliation. In erotic terms, masochism. And the shoe or the boot stands for the foot, and may have as much erotic interest for the subject as the foot itself—or more. And that casts an interesting light on the Cinderella story, doesn't it? And there's a very much earlier version of that story which is rather fascinating. An eagle is supposed to have dropped a golden sandal over Memphis, where a Pharaoh was holding a court of justice, and the man fell in love with the sandal and sent his men far and wide to discover the owner. And it turned out to be the hetaira Rhodope, who lived in the city of Naucratis, and they brought her along to Memphis and Pharaoh married her. And I suppose they lived happily ever after."

"It was a golden sandal you lost, wasn't it?" Simon said. "So perhaps an eagle flew off with it."

"Well, my Pharaoh is arriving this morning, bringing

some more shoes and taking me out to lunch," Vivien said, getting up, "so I suppose I'd better get dressed properly."

"Just a minute," Christine said, still following her own line of thought. "You'd say, in simple terms, that á foot fetishist is someone who falls in love with shoes."

"That's about it," she agreed.

"Passionately? I mean, can it be a violent sort of emotion?"

"I suppose so. I can't say I've ever known one personally, so I haven't had the chance to get him to unburden himself to me. But I'll tell you someone who's probably got the aberration in a small way, and that's your friend, Mrs. Maskell. Remember her collection of china shoes that she wanted me to go over and see today? Some of those will have been made as fetishist objects. But I don't suppose for a moment she's got the faintest idea of the fact."

"What I wanted to know," Christine said, "is whether the emotion can be so strong that a person might go to great lengths to acquire an unusual collection of shoes, like the ones you've got here? In other words, if Simon mightn't be right."

Vivien laughed. "I couldn't tell you."

"How many people knew you'd have that collection of shoes here with you?" Simon asked.

"Quite a lot, I suppose," Vivien said. "All the members of the Helsington Costume Society, to begin with."

"But most of them wouldn't know when there was a chance of getting into your room."

"You're saying," Christine said, "that someone in this house, who could watch for a moment when Vivien's room would be empty, went into her room, got the wrong shoes, gave them to someone outside, who was so angry at being given the wrong lot that he threw them into the fire, and then told his accomplice in the house to go back and get the right lot. But he couldn't get into Vivien's room to do it, because by then she was in it herself, lying down. And of course there's only one person who could be the accomplice, and that's Lew, who turned up, just by coincidence, the evening before Vivien. But why should he murder his mother? And why should he hide in the storeroom? And even if he did, and she found him there, it wouldn't worry her."

"Suppose it wasn't Lew who was the accomplice," Simon said, "but Mrs. Heacham herself."

"And then she was murdered by the person she'd helped— why?" Christine asked. "So that she couldn't betray his eccentricity?"

Vivien laughed again. "You've both of you been reading too many of the wrong sort of books. There's no need to connect my shoes being stolen with the murder. The shoes were taken by that beastly little boy, and Mrs. Heacham— well, my guess is Lew killed her, because he's a completely unbalanced person, even if that doesn't show very much, or because she refused him money, or something like that. Now I'm going upstairs to dress."

When she had gone, Simon said sombrely, "She could be right, you know."

"About Lew?"

"About Lew and David and that you and I read the wrong sort of books."

"I hardly read at all," Christine said. She stretched out comfortably on the sofa, arranging a cushion under her head. "Do you know, when Mrs. Heacham first came to us, and I still had Linda Deeping, and then we got Marsha, I kept thinking this is simply wonderful, I'm going to do all the reading I've promised myself I'd do some day when I had time, and I'll write, and I'll paint, and I'll take up machine embroidery or something? And in fact, I never have any more time than I had before. I don't read, I don't write, I don't do anything special. I haven't even done anything about the garden. It's still the dreary waste it's always been."

Simon sat down at the end of the sofa and absent-mindedly stroked her ankles.

"Tell me about Marsha," he said.

"What about her?" Christine asked.

"Everything."

"Yes—well—if you'd just indicate what interests you particularly . . ."

"I told you, everything."

"For instance, is she as good as she is beautiful, like the Princess in the fairy story?"

"More or less."

"Isn't that something for you to find out for yourself?" she suggested.

"Yes, of course," he agreed, "but you see, I want to talk about her. Just that. Talk and think about her. I don't mind much what we say as long as we don't get too far away from the subject. Praise, criticise, it really doesn't signify, as long as I can say her name from time to time. It gives me a good feeling just to hear it."

Christine drew her feet up under her. "Well, she's kind, she's affectionate, she's intelligent—"

"I wasn't asking for a reference."

"What were you asking for, then?"

He laughed and said, "You know as well as I do. To hear myself talking about her, as I said. You can stay absolutely mute, if you want to."

"Oh, Simon dear," she said, "what a pity it is you know as much about yourself as you do. You kill every emotion you have that might mean something important stone dead before it's had time to come to anything simply by posturing about it. If you've fallen in love with Marsha, why can't you keep it to yourself and let the steam work up inside you till it really blows you up?"

"I've been blown up in the past," he said. "I didn't really enjoy the experience."

"I don't believe you for a moment, if you're talking about you and me," she said. "That idea's just a convenient defence. Mind you, I enjoy it. When one's middle-aged and happily married, it just rounds things off nicely to have another man incurably in love with one. If you marry Marsha, and she doesn't understand the fiction, I shall miss you. But honestly, I think it's time you grew out of it."

"Would Marsha marry me, do you think?"

"Today? Tomorrow? No. I don't think she's the kind to be rushed. But if you were to work at it . . ."

"But there's this chap, Rodney Maskell, hanging around. What does she think about him?"

"I think that he's just an oaf. A nice one, but still an oaf."

"What about Lew then?"

"He's probably a crook."

"You think so?" he said. "You really think Lew's a crook?"

"Officially, in the sense that he's ever been convicted of anything, I haven't the faintest idea," she answered. "Perhaps Mr. Ditteridge will tell us sometime. I mean, if Lew's got a record."

"Will he benefit by his mother's death?"

"I don't think so."

"Of course, you realise that Henry and I are going to."

"Benefit—Henry and you?"

"Yes, the capital that was set aside to give her that pension of hers will be divided between us now."

"It can't be much."

"I think it was five thousand."

"Less tax."

"As you say, less tax."

"Simon, I can't see anyone believing that you or Henry committed a murder for two thousand five hundred, less tax," Christine said. "To go back to Marsha..."

"Yes?"

She stood up and patted his shoulder. "She's all that I was starting to say she was when you interrupted. She's a warmhearted, loving sort of person. But also she seems to have pretty clear ideas about where she's going in life, so fooling around won't get you anywhere. And if you just manage to make her unhappy, I'll be very angry with you. I think she's a very promising sort of human being, who ought to be given the best possible chance in life. Now I'd better go out and investigate the food situation. It's just dawned on me that lunch isn't going to appear of itself today. I'll have to do something about it."

She went out to the kitchen.

There were plentiful signs there that the police had been in occupation. Teacups with dregs of tea in them were on the table, with cigarette stubs and ash in the saucers. The sink basket was full of tea leaves. A freshly opened packet of sweet biscuits was almost empty. Linda Deeping had been dispensing hospitality for the family. She was in the kitchen now by herself, seated at the table, drinking instant coffee, and smoking a cigarette. Sounds from the storeroom told Christine that there were still policemen in there.

"Would you like some coffee?" Linda asked. "The kettle's still hot. I can make it in a minute."

"No, thank you," Christine said. "I just came out to see what I can do about lunch, though I don't suppose anyone's going to be awfully hungry."

"Yes, it does kind of take the edge off your appetite, a thing like this," Linda said. "I still feel shaky. Joe's ever so angry with me for the way I carried on. Screaming and all!"

"I'd have screamed myself if I'd opened a trunk and found what you did," Christine said.

"Joe didn't scream," Linda replied. "I can't think of anything that'd make him scream. He hasn't any nerves. Nothing upsets him. Not things like dead bodies and such. He'd have been upset all right last night if he'd been at the party I went to, but he was on the evening shift, so he didn't know anything about it." She pushed her pink hair back from her face. "I don't usually go to parties by myself. When I knew Joe was going to be on the late shift, I rang up and said I couldn't go. It was being given by one of the other young constables and his wife. I don't hardly know them, really, but they're nice. They said why didn't I come by myself and Joe could come on and join me when he was free. And Joe said, 'Yes, why don't you go, Linda?' So I said, 'Oh, I'd feel out of place.' All the same, I went. And when I got there, everyone was dancing, and there was couples in all the corners, with men making love to other men's wives—it was that sort of party. I began to feel glad Joe hadn't come. He doesn't like that sort of thing. So I sat by myself on a sofa, and a young man came up to me and said, 'Linda, would you like to dance?' So we danced once or twice. Then ever so casually, he says to me, 'Have you ever had a love affair, Linda?' I said, 'What d'you mean?' 'A love affair,' he says, 'would you like to, because if you would, I wouldn't mind.' He wouldn't *mind*, he said. I said, 'Thank you, I'm married and very happily, as it happens.'

'Oh well,' he says, 'I just thought you might like to, most married women do nowadays.' Can you imagine? I suppose I should've told him off, only he wasn't *rude* or anything. It was just like he was asking if I'd like another drink."

She stood up and began collecting cups and saucers and stacking them beside the dishwasher, ready for Christine to put them into it. She had never come to terms with the dishwasher herself, and preferred to do any washing up that she did by hand.

"And now I don't know when Joe'll be able to paint the storeroom," she said. "He thought he could put in most of today on it, and at least get the old paint scraped down. But next week he's on the dayshift, so he won't be free while there's light."

If Joe was on the day shift next week, that meant that Linda would be bringing her four-year-old, Maureen, with her, as Joe would not be at home to look after her. This would please Frances, who was a very motherly little girl, and liked having Maureen to play with, better than any of her toys.

Christine opened the dishwasher to put in the cups and saucers. But she found that it was still full of last night's crockery and would have to be emptied first. The routine in the household with the washing up was that after dinner Marsha would fill the dishwasher, press the knob and leave it to work, then next morning, after breakfast, Mrs. Heacham would empty it, wash the filters, refill the machine with the breakfast things, leaving these till the lunch things had been added to them, to set it running again. When Henry and Christine had been living alone, they had been able to get through a whole day on only one washing, but with their increased household, they had to do it twice. And this morning, of course, no one had thought of emptying the dishwasher at all. Not that it contained any dinner plates, as Henry and Christine had been out, but the things that Marsha and Lew had used for their meal were there.

Christine began to take out the silver and the glasses. Then she paused.

It was a small thing. A small, domestic thing that she might easily have missed. It was just by chance that it caught her eye.

When Mrs. Heacham put her supper on the tray to take up to her bedroom, she always used a blue and white mug for her milk. It had somehow become her own personal property. And it was not in the dishwasher.

Nor, when Christine looked, was the blue earthenware eggcup that she used for her egg.

Christine could not tell if her plate, knife, and eggspoon were there, because they matched the other things in the dishwasher. She could not tell either at first what it meant that the mug and the eggcup were missing. But after a moment's thought she shut the dishwasher again without emptying it, left the kitchen and went upstairs, all the way upstairs to the floor that Mrs. Heacham had always referred to as the attics.

In the doorway of Mrs. Heacham's room she met Joe Deeping.

"I'm sorry, Mrs. Findon," he said, "but the Superintendent doesn't want anyone to come in here."

"Then can you just tell me something?" Christine said. "Is Mrs. Heacham's supper tray in there?"

"Supper tray?" he said.

"Yes, a tray with a blue and white mug on it and a blue eggcup, perhaps with an egg in it, or perhaps just an egg shell."

He shook his head. "There's no tray here at all, Mrs. Findon."

"You're sure?"

"You can see for yourself," he said, stepping to one side so that she could see all round the room without going in.

She had very seldom seen the room since Mrs. Heacham had taken it over. She had had a right to her privacy, Christine had thought, and had not gone in without an invitation. There had not been many of these. They had been issued only when something was wrong. For instance, when a light bulb had failed, Mrs. Heacham had not liked climbing onto a chair to replace it and would ask Henry or Christine to come to the rescue. Once a sash cord had broken and she had asked Christine in to show it to her so that she would call the joiner. Once or twice she had been unwell and Christine had taken her meals up to her.

It was a room that had never failed to strike a chill to her heart. In itself it was reasonably pleasant. It had a fitted, dark green carpet, white walls, some light oak furniture that dated from the early days of the Findons' marriage and had not cost much but was not unattractive, cheerful flowered curtains, a red and green bedspread, and, of course, a television. But such things as pictures, books in the small bookcase, and china knickknacks, they had assumed that Mrs. Heacham would prefer to choose for herself. But she had added nothing. The room was as impersonal as on the day that she had moved in. A big framed photograph of Henry's father was the only ornament. There were no photographs of Lew, even in infancy, or of her husband. Ornaments, Mrs. Heachman had once said to Christine, when she had offered her a choice of a few for which there seemed to be no place downstairs, only collect dust. Christine had sometimes felt that Mrs. Heacham had been doing her best to turn the room into the barren attic that she had called it, and that she would have felt more satisfied with it if there had been worn linoleum on the floor, a broken blind at the window, and a bed with broken springs and a sagging mattress, instead of the good foam rubber one that had been given to her. That would have assuaged her grievance against life, made her feel that her grudge against them all was justified.

"The tray," Joe Deeping said, "is there something about it?"

"I'm not sure," Christine said. "I must think."

She went downstairs again.

She found Henry in their bedroom. He had not exactly made the bed, because he did not know quite how to do it properly, but he had roughly straightened the sheets and blankets, thrown the bedspread over them, and had lain down on it with his hands folded under his head. His dinner jacket and the other things that he had worn the evening before were scattered about the room. As a rule he was moderately kind to his clothes, but as a part of his protest at having to dress at all to go out, he afterwards always maltreated everything that he had had to wear as if he were punishing the unfortunate things for the trouble that they had been to him. Recognising the situation, Christine got a hanger from the wardrobe and began to arrange his dinner jacket and trousers on it.

She did not ask him what he was doing in the bedroom. With policemen in his study, Simon in the sitting room, Linda Deeping in the kitchen, and more policemen in other parts of the house, this room was the obvious place to take refuge.

When she had hung up his suit, she sat down at the end of the bed.

"A funny thing's happened." she said.

He had been looking more or less at her as she moved about, but a long way through her. She now saw him try to focus on her face.

"On the whole," he said, "it *is* what you might call a very funny murder."

"That's how it strikes me. But listen, Henry, you know we've all been thinking Mrs. Heacham must have been killed some time after we went out."

"Well, wasn't she?"

"I'm not at all sure that she was."

"Why not?"

"Her mug and her eggcup aren't in the dishwasher, and they aren't up in her room either."

"And what does that mean?"

"I think it means she never got her supper at all."

"Why?"

"Well, what she usually did in the evenings was get her supper, put it on a tray and take it up to her room and watch television while she ate it. Then some time later on, when she felt like it, she'd bring the tray downstairs again and put the mug and other things into the dishwasher, and then Marsha added the dinner things when we'd had dinner, and ran the thing, and left it for Mrs. Heacham to empty in the morning. So this morning, naturally, it hasn't been emptied. But Mrs. Heacham's mug and eggcup aren't there."

"And you think that means she was killed before she got her supper, while all the rest of us were still in the house?"

"Doesn't it?"

"It could. On the other hand, yesterday wasn't a normal day for her. She'd got Lew on her hands. Suppose she thought she'd like to have supper with him when the rest of us were out of the way. She might have gone up to her room and waited till we'd all gone, then come down to look for him, and just happened on the time when he and Roddie were out with Marsha. And she heard a noise in the storeroom and went in and that was that."

"Mmm . . . yes . . . You think that's likelier, do you, than what I was thinking?"

"I don't know about likelier. Just possible also."

"But ought I to tell Mr. Ditteridge about it?"

"Oh, of course."

She began to stand up. Henry's hand shot out and caught her by the arm.

"Wait a minute," he said. "Don't go."

She was going to sit down again where she had been sitting before, at the foot of the bed, but he drew her closer to him.

"What is it?" she asked.

"Nothing," he answered. "Nothing special."

"But oughtn't I to—?"

"It can wait a few minutes, can't it? Can't we just have a few minutes together, on our own?" He sounded almost sulky, as if she were to blame for that morning's invasion of their home. "We never seem to have any time to ourselves nowadays."

"I know," she said with a sigh. "But today doesn't seem the best possible time to start trying to organise it. Anyway, the children aren't here forever, and Marsha will go when they go, and Lew will probably remove himself fairly soon—"

"If the police don't remove him for us first."

"Yes, and Vivien's moving out today, because Barry's coming down to give her moral support, and they're going to stay at the Crown, and . . ." It felt too cold-blooded to say that the problem of Mrs. Heacham had solved itself, so she skipped that. "And Simon will go back to London as soon as the police let him go."

"Simon—yes." Henry said it thoughtfully. Suddenly he reached out for her and pulled her down on the bed beside him and held her tight. "Christine, do you ever regret that you didn't marry Simon?"

"Yes," she said, "every time I see the gas bill."

"No," he said and his voice actually shook. "Don't laugh at me. Answer me. Tell me the truth."

"You know the truth, don't you?"

"But say it."

She pressed her cheek against his, then they were kissing, a long kiss, quiet and satisfying. When they drew apart, he still kept hold of her.

"Go on, say it," he insisted.

"But why today, all of a sudden?" she said. "I've never regretted it, and you know it, and I don't think you've ever asked me about it all these years."

"I've thought about it, all the same," he said.

"But why?"

"Because when I see you together—oh, you seem to understand each other so well. You seem to match, in some way."

"And d'you mean you've been worrying . . . ?"

There was worry for once in those innocent-looking eyes of his, which saw so much more than one expected.

"At times," he said.

"Then it must be because you want to worry sometimes," she said, "to propitiate the fates that gave us each other."

"That could be true, perhaps. But if you'd married Simon, you'd have minks and diamonds by now. Don't you ever think about that?"

"Well, I'd like some minks and diamonds—yes," she said. "I won't deny it. They help to place one high in the pecking order. But when you say something like that, I know you aren't worrying seriously. You're just indulging a mood of self-pity or something. So to go back to what I asked you, why today, all of a sudden?"

"I suppose because it's dawned on me how little we've been seeing of each other lately," he answered, "and how

I took our old peace and quiet for granted. And that's started me wondering if that peace and quiet was what you wanted, or if this sort of thing is what you've always hankered after. Have I, that's to say, been blind and self-satisfied?"

"A murder a day keeps boredom away!"

"I wasn't actually thinking about the murder. I was thinking about Simon, and whether or not his kind of life wouldn't have suited you far better than what you've had with me."

"Seeing that I didn't have children," she said. "That's what you're edging up to, isn't it?"

"Well—yes."

"Look," she said, "I love these children and I love Simon. But if you want the sober truth, I love them ever so much more when I don't have to see too much of them. And I'll tell you something about Simon. I think I may not be the centre of his life much longer. Not that I ever really have been. That's just a kind of game we've played. I always thought you understood that. Anyway, I think he's been hit hard by our Marsha. I really do. He's being flippant about it, but for once I saw a gleam of fear in his eye, as if he were really afraid of being swept out of his depth."

Henry shook his head. "That's just the matchmaker in you. They only met for the first time yesterday."

"I think if Simon ever really falls in love with anybody, it's going to be at first sight, and then he'll be married in a week."

"Not to Marsha. You're forgetting, she'll consider it immoral to marry him unless they've slept together first."

"Well, a lot can happen in a week."

They both started laughing. But laughter sounded out of place in the house that morning and they stopped at once. Christine got off the bed, crossed to the dressing-table and combed her hair.

"I'd better go and tell Mr. Ditteridge about Mrs. Heacham's supper things now," she said.

"All right, I'll come along too."

They went downstairs together.

# 7

They were just in time to see a covered stretcher being carried out through the front door to the waiting ambulance. The end of Mrs. Heacham. Christine came as near to feeling grief for her then as she was ever going to be able, and that grief was really for herself, for Henry, for the children, for all of them, because one day they would all go the same way, and heaven knew if by then there would be anyone there to sorrow over them or not.

Lew watched the stretcher carried out, then gave a harsh cry and looked as if he were going to fling himself after it. But Simon was there, caught him by the shoulders and guided him into the sitting room. Through the open front door Christine saw that a small crowd had gathered on the pavement, standing there patiently, as if waiting for a glimpse of a celebrity. Mr. Ditteridge stood in the doorway, watching as the stretcher was slid into the ambulance and the ambulance drove off. Then he turned back into the house and closed the door behind him.

"Mr. Ditteridge," Christine said, "there's something odd I'd like to tell you about Mrs. Heacham's supper things."

He had to bring his attention back from a distance to focus on her. She did not know what he had been thinking about. Perhaps just death itself, as she had been. Or perhaps some important clue that he had dug out of his questioning

of Lew, or even Simon, or Vivien. Or perhaps he was
feeling hungry and had been considering where he might
have some lunch soon. Or perhaps his thoughts had been
on Pippy, and on what a cosy, comforting little thing she
was in a harsh world, so ferocious to everyone else, so
tender to him.

"Yes?" he said.

"If you'd come to the kitchen," Christine said, "I can
explain."

He followed her to the kitchen. Henry followed him.
Vivien, who had been in the sitting room with Simon and
Lew, realised that something was happening and followed
too. She had dressed in the dark brown suit in which she
had arrived, and had her short mink jacket over her arm,
and was waiting, Christine supposed, for Barry to arrive in
their car to pick her up and take her to the Crown.

Christine opened the dishwasher, meaning to demonstrate
what she meant about the mug and eggcup.

The dishwasher was empty.

Linda Deeping, who was in the kitchen, peeling potatoes,
on the assumption that they were bound to want potatoes
sooner or later, whether anyone had said so or not, and
needing something to do, observed, "She come and emptied
it—Miss Lindale."

"Well, I can still explain," Christine said, and did so.
She ended, "But my husband and I disagree about what it
means that the things weren't there. I think it means—I
think it *may* mean—that Mrs. Heacham heard something
suspicious in the storeroom quite early, and went in there
to investigate and got killed before we ever left the house.
But my husband thinks that for once Mrs. Heacham put off
having her supper, so that she could have it later with Lew,
and that it was when everyone else was out of the house
that she heard the noise in the storeroom and went in."

Mr. Ditteridge nodded, tugged thoughtfully at his lower
lip, eyed the empty dishwasher and said, "But whatever it
may mean, you're sure, are you, Mrs. Findon, that Mrs.
Heacham's usual supper things weren't here?"

"Quite sure," she said, "but you could check it with Miss
Lindale."

"That's right," he said, but still with that air that he had had as he had watched Mrs. Heacham's body carried out of thinking of something else. He sent one of the constables to fetch Marsha. "What still puzzles me most," he went on, while they were waiting for her, "is the motive for this murder. Doesn't it puzzle you?" He was addressing them all. "Not so much when, as why."

Henry nodded. "Only a little while ago I was telling my wife I found this a funny murder. That's what I meant. If Mrs. Heacham was killed because she interrupted something in the storeroom, what could she conceivably have interrupted? If it was someone who'd come in from outside, why hasn't anything been stolen? If it was one of us here in the house, what was that person doing in the storeroom? I suppose there's no doubt she was killed in the storeroom, is there? There's no chance she was killed somewhere else and put there afterwards?"

Mr. Ditteridge shook his head. "There are the blood spots that begin just inside the door, and none outside. And the floor in there's pretty dusty, and there's dust on her knees and her skirt, as if she went down in there. No, that's where it happened. But why, Mr. Findon, why?"

With quick steps Marsha came in, and as if drawn by a magnet, Simon appeared at her elbow.

"Have I done something wrong?" Marsha asked, looking apprehensive. "What is it?"

"Will you ask Miss Lindale about it, Mrs. Findon?" Mr. Ditteridge said. "It'll help me get it straight in my own mind."

"Did you empty the dishwasher this morning, Marsha?" Christine asked.

"Yes, I—I just thought I might help," she said. "I mean, Mrs. Heacham usually did it, and she—well, nobody'd done it, so I—I just did it. Was it wrong?"

"It was very thoughtful," Simon said at once. "It couldn't possibly have been wrong."

"But can you remember, when you emptied it," Christine said, "if Mrs. Heacham's blue and white mug and blue eggcup were in it? That's all we want to know."

"Oh, I don't know," Marsha answered, sounding bewildered and still slightly scared. "I wasn't thinking much about what I was doing. I just had the feeling I ought to be doing something. Yes, I think it was there—no, it wasn't. Oh, I don't know, I really don't know!"

"But if you think hard—"

Simon interrupted, "Don't bully her, Christine! How would you like to be asked a thing like that all of a sudden— I mean, about some quite trivial thing, which no one would have noticed in the circumstances? It's most unfair."

"I'm not bullying anyone," Christine answered. "I'm simply asking, can she remember if there was a mug and an eggcup in the dishwasher when she emptied it? What's unfair about that?"

He moved closer to Marsha, as if to protect her.

"It's very difficult to remember anything clearly when one isn't prepared to be asked about it," he said. "Don't let it worry you, Marsha. Just take your time."

"I honestly don't know," she said. "I just took everything out of the dishwasher and put it away. I didn't think about what was there."

Christine turned to Mr. Ditteridge. "But *I* know what was there, Superintendent. I know the mug and the eggcup weren't there."

"Yes, yes," he said. "Just so. I'm sure I can accept your statement, Mrs. Findon. I don't doubt it in the least. What it means, of course, as you pointed out yourself, is another matter."

"I'm so sorry I'm so stupid," Marsha said. "I'm really awfully sorry."

"Not at all, Miss Lindale," Mr. Ditteridge said. "Much better to say you aren't sure about a thing than to come up with a flat statement one way or the other that might not be true."

"The only intelligent thing to do," Simon said. "Now are we finished in here, or is there any other way we can help?"

Mr. Ditteridge hesitated for a moment, then said that that was all for the present. One after the other, they all left the kitchen.

Christine went upstairs again to the bedroom, and started

to remake the bed. Henry's shirt, black tie, black socks, and patent leather shoes were still all in different parts of the room. His cuff links were still in the cuffs of the shirt. She had just picked up the socks, and was holding them vaguely, meaning to take them to the linen basket in the bathroom, when the telephone rang.

She picked up the extension by the bed, but Henry, downstairs, was already answering the call. She heard him say their number, then heard Minna Maskell's voice say, "Henry? It's Minna. It's just that I was wondering whether or not you were coming over for drinks. You remember, we talked about it last night, so I thought I'd ring up to find out."

"Great heavens, Minna," Henry answered. "I'm afraid we completely forgot about letting you know. Unforgiveable. We ought to have telephoned. But there's a great deal wrong here. We found Mrs. Heacham dead this morning. And it's murder. Some prowler, we suppose, who got in last night while we were all out. And we've had the police here all the morning."

"Murder—oh, my God!" Minna squealed. "In *your* house?"

Christine broke in on the conversation.

"Minna—I'm so sorry, of course we should have telephoned, but we've none of us been ourselves today. But Vivien's sure to visit us again and she can see your collection then."

"Oh, my collection . . . !" Minna dismissed it. "But did you ever find what happened to Mrs. Richmond's own shoes? Not that you'll have been thinking about that either with a murder on your hands. A murder—oh, my God! Tony—" She was calling to her husband. "Can you believe it, that poor Mrs. Heacham was murdered by a prowler in the Findons' house last night?"

Christine was almost certain that she heard Tony Maskell give his little titter in the background.

Minna went on, "My dears, if there's anything we can do—anything—I mean, for instance, take the children off your hands for the day. Would that be a help? It must be a terrible atmosphere for them to be in. I could send Roddie round with the car to collect them. And that nice girl, Marsha, too, as they're accustomed to her."

Almost as one, Christine and Henry replied that it was immensely kind of Minna, and just like her, and that they were tremendously grateful, but that they doubted very much if the police would let anyone go.

Minna said, "Well, anything else you may think of later, just ask. I mean—oh, my God, a murder! Do you think it really was a prowler, or was it that odd son of Mrs. Heacham's? Roddie said he didn't take to him at all, in fact, he felt quite uneasy, letting Marsha drive off with him . . . Drive off!" Her voice rose shrilly. "Is that when it happened—I mean, when the three of them were out in the car? Roddie told me how they'd driven him home, and I felt quite uneasy even then at the thought of the three of them driving off like that, leaving the children with just Mrs. Heacham in the house. But if that was when it happened, of course it couldn't have been the son. Well, I won't keep you any longer, but remember if there's anything I can do . . . Oh, I've just thought of something. About Mrs. Richmond's shoes. Do you think the murderer could have stolen them to make a false footprint somewhere? I mean, suppose the murderer really had rather large feet, and he— or was it, she?—wanted to mislead everyone, and so deliberately made a footprint somewhere with one of Mrs. Richmond's shoes."

"In that case, why take four shoes?" Henry said. "Wouldn't one have been enough?"

"Perhaps just to make things more puzzling. You might suggest it to the police, anyway, in case they haven't thought of it. Good-bye now, my dears. Tony and I are feeling so shaken by your news, we must have a drink, even if you aren't here to have it with us."

She rang off. Christine put the telephone down, picked up Henry's shirt and started taking the cuff links out of it.

The door opened and Marsha came in.

"Are you very busy?" she asked. "Can I talk to you for a minute or two?"

She was looking both uneasy and downcast. In fact, Christine thought that she had been crying. There was a touch of red about her eyelids, while the rest of her flower-petal face was unusually pale.

"Another time will do, if you're too busy," she added diffidently.

"No, I'm just looking for things to do to keep me occupied." Christine sat down in a chair. "Come in and shut the door. What's the trouble?"

Marsha advanced a step or two, closing the door behind her.

"Do you want me to leave?" she asked abruptly.

"Leave? What ever's put that into your head?"

"But do you want me to?"

"No, why should I?"

"Because of last night."

"Going out, you mean?"

"Yes, and leaving the children. It was a breach of trust."

"That's a solemn way of putting it—though I admit I'd just as soon it didn't happen again. I can be sure it won't, can't I?"

"Oh, absolutely. That is . . ." Marsha took hold of a lock of her fair hair and coiled it round a finger. "*I* can be sure it won't, but whether you'll ever feel sure yourself . . . I mean, I can promise, but if you didn't believe the promise, I'd understand. I know I oughtn't to have gone out. It was just that it seemed the quickest way of getting rid of Roddie, and I never meant to stop for that drink. And then this morning, the way I let you down over what was in the dishwasher. I must have sounded so stupid and unhelpful. But I honestly couldn't remember what I'd taken out of it. One does that sort of thing so automatically."

"Of course one does," Christine said. "Anyway, I'm quite sure myself Mrs. Heacham's things weren't in it. If anyone doesn't believe me, that's not your fault." She began to fiddle with Henry's cuff links again. "Marsha, are you really trying to nerve yourself to say you want to go?"

"Oh, no, no, no!" she cried, and her eyes misted with tears. "I love it here. I've been so happy. You're all so nice

to me. I just dread the time when I'll have to go away. And
I started knitting that sweater for you yesterday, just to try
to show you how much I appreciated everything."

"Well, that's nice..." Christine paused. She was not
looking at Marsha, but at the shirt cuff from which she was
trying to extract the cuff link. Along the fold of the cuff
was a smear of dull brownish red. Blood. It could not have
been anything else. But why on Henry's cuff? Had he
scratched or pricked himself the evening before?

Suddenly from downstairs came the sound of a shout.

The extraordinary thing about it was that the voice was
Henry's and Henry was never much given to shouting.

Christine heard what he shouted quite distinctly. "What
the hell are you doing with that?"

She dropped the shirt, jumped up and ran to the door.
Marsha had swung round and was through it ahead of her.
Looking down the stairs they saw an astonishing sight.

David stood in the middle of the hall. He was dressed
in his usual jeans and jersey. But on one foot he had a shoe
of green silk damask with a silver buckle and a high red
heel. In one hand he was holding the black cane with the
ivory handle that Vivien had used in her masquerade the
evening before, and in the other a snuffbox, Henry's most
treasured one, a gold one with a monogram in rubies on the
lid. Posing there, like a gouty old dandy, David hobbled
a step or two forward, smiling up at Henry, who was in the
doorway of the sitting room, then tucked the cane under his
arm, opened the snuffbox and helped himself to an imag-
inary pinch of snuff.

"Egad!" he said. "Odd's fish! By my hallidom!"

For once Henry looked really angry. No one but he and
Christine was allowed to open the cabinet where the snuffboxes were. Besides that, David must have rifled Vivien's
suitcase to get the green damask shoe, and there had been
enough trouble already over Vivien's shoes.

But before Henry had thought of what to say to express
his anger, Lew thrust past him out of the sitting room,
grasped David by the shoulder, stared at him, then burst
into a bellow of high laughter.

"You're a bright one!" Lew cried on a shrill, sobbing

note of hysteria. "You've just told me what happened. You've told me everything!"

Still laughing wildly, he let David go, turned to the stairs and raced up them, thrust past Christine and Marsha, and went pounding up the stairs to the attics.

What ought they to have done?

It came into Christine's head as they stood there that sometime she must tell David that he had mixed up his periods a little. "By my hallidom!" did not go with snuff-boxes and red-heeled shoes. Apart from that she could not think of anything to say to him.

Even Henry, who was so much more used to children than she was, seemed to have nothing more to say after his first explosion of wrath. It was as if he felt that it was far more important to understand Lew's outburst than to scold David, while Christine felt that she wanted to comfort him rather than to scold him, because another of his jokes had gone wrong. And jokes that fall flat are so very hurtful to the self-esteem. He looked as if he were getting ready to cry.

But to be faced with having to discipline a young child in a house where a murder had taken place was very confusing. What David had done was irritating, out of place, absurd, but so innocent. Or seemed so. Because of course what Lew had said about David having told him everything was nonsense. Wasn't it? There could be no sinister meaning behind David's little bit of dressing up and acting.

After a moment Henry said quietly, "Give me those things, David, then go upstairs and try not to be a nuisance. We haven't time for this sort of thing today."

Silently David took off the green shoe and handed it to Henry with the cane and the snuffbox. Turning to Vivien, who was behind him in the doorway of the sitting room, Henry handed her the shoe.

"I'm sorry about this, Vivien," he said, "but it doesn't seem the time to make a fuss."

For once she did not seem to want to make a fuss. She hardly glanced at the shoe as she took it. She was looking up the stairs after Lew.

"What did he mean?" she asked.

"Nothing that makes any sense to me," Henry answered. He turned to Mr. Ditteridge, who had watched the scene without saying anything. "Does it to you, Superintendent?"

Mr. Ditteridge looked withdrawn and thoughtful. He spoke to David. "What about you, young fellow? Had you any bright ideas in your head when you took those things?"

"No," David muttered.

"There's nothing you saw yesterday, or heard, that you were—well, acting for us?"

"No, no, no!" David shouted at him and bolted up the stairs.

"What *could* he have been acting?" Vivien said. "My guess is, Lew's the one who's acting. He acts a good deal of the time, doesn't he?"

"I'll go up and talk to David," Christine said. "I'll see if he'll tell me anything. But I think Vivien's right, it's Lew who put on the real show."

"But why?" she asked.

"He likes to have attention on himself," Christine said.

But as she went up the stairs she wondered if what Lew really wanted was to distract attention from himself. He was in a very difficult position in the household, and perhaps had had just about enough time to become frightened for himself, to wonder when they were all going to start thinking of him as a possible murderer. To act as if he had suddenly been vouchsafed insight through David's play-acting into what had happened here last night might be clever tactics.

She found David and Frances in their playroom, doing a strange sort of dance together, in which they encircled Christine, swooping around her with wild gestures and war whoops. They were trying to work off the tension left behind by the scene downstairs. She waited a little while, till she saw some of the excitement beginning to subside.

"All right, now that's that," she said. "Suppose you calm down and tell me what all that was about."

"It wasn't about anything," Frances said happily. "We were just having fun."

"I don't mean the dance," Christine said. "I meant the dressing up."

She sat down. Frances came and leant against her and gave her a light kiss on the temple.

"I meant the dressing up," she said. "At home we do a lot of dressing up. Sometimes I dress up as an Indian lady in a sari Daddy brought home to Mummy once when he went abroad, and sometimes I dress up as a cowboy. That used to be David's—the hat and the belt and the gun and all—but they're too small for him now, so I wear them. And sometimes I wear a silver star in my hair, that came off a Christmas tree and Mummy's nightgown, then I'm queen of the fairies."

"Fairies!" David said darkly. "She believes in fairies!"

"I don't, I don't!" Frances cried, and leaving Christine, leapt at him, butting him hard in the stomach. He reeled under the impact, but managed to keep his feet, twisting away from her, then grabbing a handful of her hair and holding it tightly enough to immobilize her.

"Fairies, fairies, she believes in fairies!" he sang at her mockingly.

She squealed so piercingly that he let her go.

"I do *not* believe in fairies," she said with dignity. "I don't believe in anything."

"That's only what she says," David explained. "You try telling her anything you like and she'll believe you. Make up the silliest thing you can think of and she'll swallow it whole."

"Like what?" Christine asked.

"Well, like saying I know who killed Mrs. Heacham," he answered.

Christine felt a little breathless. "Do you know that, David?"

He went into fits of laughter. "I caught you, didn't I?" he cried. "You thought I knew!" He began to dance about the room again.

She caught at him when he came near and drew him to her.

"Listen, David," she said, "listen carefully. You mustn't say that sort of thing if you don't mean it. Do you understand?"

"But it wasn't a lie," he said. "I didn't tell you a lie. I was just pretending."

"All right, you were pretending," she said, "and that doesn't matter, only there are some things you mustn't pretend about, and one of them is Mrs. Heacham. Promise me you won't."

"Why?" he asked.

She began to feel frightened. She did not dare to say because it could possibly, just possibly, be dangerous. She had not even thought, until that moment, that it could be.

"Will you promise just because I ask you to?" she asked, not very hopefully.

"*I* will," Frances at once said generously.

David took a little longer to say, "All right. But we don't know anything, you know. Really we don't. Please don't be unhappy." With one of his quicksilver changes of mood, he was suddenly concerned about her. "Would you like to read my novel, Christine? If you'd like to, you may, only you must promise me faithfully you'll never tell a living soul about it."

"Your—?" She remembered what he had been writing yesterday, and his extreme secretiveness about it. "It would be a privilege," she said.

He fetched the exercise book in which he had been writing and handed it to her with a very false air of unconcern.

"It's just silly, of course," he said. "It isn't about anything." Then he snatched it back from her. "You must promise first, solemnly, cross your heart, you'll never tell anyone a single word about it. Then I'll promise about Mrs. Heacham."

"But suppose I like it," Christine said, "can't I tell anyone then?"

"Well . . ." He hesitated, half avid and half frightened, like any grown-up author. "I'll think about it." He gave the book back to her.

It took her about seven minutes to read the story. David had big, clear handwriting, which flowed on steadily, page after page, the story only coming to an end, it was plain, when the book was full.

It would have been nice for Christine to have been able

to say that she recognised signs of genius. But all she recognised were bits and pieces from television, particularly
Westerns, some adventure stories that he had been reading
recently, and some James Bond, though the hero was not
a man but an Alsatian dog. The best things to be said about
the story were that the style was extremely economical, that
there was a certain hurtling speed about the narrative, and
that there was a distinct freshness about the conclusion. For
one of the characters, a rustler, had been very helpful to
the Alsatian, and the final words were "So they went to the
police station, and the good rustler told the police everything
he knew, and lived happily ever after."

By the time that she had come to the end, David was
kneeling on the window seat, staring out into the garden,
his back rigid with tension.

"Thank you, David," she said as she finished. "I like it
very much."

"You don't," he said.

"I do," she said. "I specially like the end."

"The end's silly."

"I think you should go on writing," she said. If he was
not going to be a genius, he might perhaps become a very
successful writer of adventure stories and be able to keep
his parents in their old age. "But about the rustler telling
everything to the police—"

"Oh, I know he wouldn't," he broke in. "He'd never
squeal. But I only had three lines left in the book."

"I was going to say," she went on cautiously, "that if
there's anything you know about last night, anything at all,
even if it's something you think is silly, it would be much
the best thing to tell the police about it."

"I said I don't know anything," he answered.

"Then why d'you think Lew said you'd told him everything?"

David frowned. "I don't know. I didn't say anything. I
didn't say anything to anybody, except 'Egad!' and all that,
and that doesn't mean anything. You saw I didn't. I just
went and got the shoe from Mrs. Richmond's room, and
the snuffbox from the study, and the cane from the hall,
and I pretended to be like one of those old men in high-

waymen stories. They always wear shoes like that, and they always take snuff and have gout and lean on canes. I wasn't thinking about Mrs. Heacham, or Lew, or anybody. I was just acting. Frances and I act a lot at home and we dress up, like she said. I don't know why Lew started shouting at me. Do you think he's mad?"

"No, but if I were you . . ." Christine hesitated. "Well, never mind," she said. "But I shouldn't do any more acting just at present, and I shouldn't talk about Mrs. Heacham, unless it's to Henry or me or the police."

"All right," David said, his manner casual again. "But I expect Lew's mad, that's what's the matter with him. You have to be sorry for mad people, do you know that? There's a mad person at home who goes along talking to himself and making faces, and Frances and I used to laugh at him and walk along behind him talking to ourselves and making faces too, and Mummy got very angry with us, because she said we were cruel and he couldn't help being mad and we ought to be sorry for him. So I don't suppose Lew can help it either and I'm very sorry for him."

"I'm sorry for him too," said Frances, the faithful echo, then made up a little song of her own, "Lew's mad, Lew's bad, Lew's sad, loopy Lew, loopy Lew!"

Christine decided to leave it at that, got up, told them that she was going to get lunch and left them to themselves.

She went to the kitchen, meaning to make a salad to go with some cold sirloin, which she knew was in the refrigerator. And they could have cheese and fruit and coffee.

The police had gone. Whether it was for the day, or merely to get themselves lunch at the Bull, she did not know. Linda Deeping had gone too. It left a curious sense of emptiness in the place.

This was not only because there were no sounds of deep voices and heavy footsteps. It was also because that familiar, small, brittle-looking figure in the nylon overall to which Christine had grown accustomed during the last year, was missing. In proportion to the power that Mrs. Heacham had had to make her presence felt in the house, she seemed able to make her absence a positive thing. That she was not there made the quiet of the kitchen feel haunted and eerie. As

Christine took a lettuce and some tomatoes out of the refrigerator, took them to the sink and began to wash them, she could almost sense the little woman at her elbow.

The front door bell rang.

It was Barry Richmond. He began by saying that he would not come in, that he could not dream of intruding at such a time, that he had only come to fetch Vivien to get her out of the way and leave the Findons in peace. It ended with him coming in for a drink, then with him and Vivien staying on for the cold beef and salad.

Barry, as usual, sat with his eyes glued to Vivien, even when he was talking to Henry or Christine, and spoke in a soft, muffled voice, almost as if he were expecting Vivien to relay to everyone else what he was saying. He had always done this during the time that the Findons had known him. A result of it was that now, after two years, they did not feel that they knew him any better than on the day when they had first met him. He seemed to use his wife as a kind of defence between the world and himself, living from choice and with a disconcerting effect of deliberation, in her shadow.

He was shorter than Vivien, fair-haired, pallid, with a smooth, unlined face with neat, unmemorable features, and he dressed with a conscientious sort of carelessness, as if he felt that this was what most of the kind of people whom he knew expected of him, although in fact he found it a considerable effort. Henry and Christine had agreed very soon after first meeting him that he was about as colourless a human being as they knew.

Yet Vivien seemed to expand when he was there. She bloomed and sparkled for him. Both of her previous husbands had been handsome men, and this had perhaps provided more competition with her own beauty than she had been able to stand, while the total lack of such competition from Barry was just what she needed. And to do him justice, he was not a stupid man. He could talk interestingly at least about his work. His real trouble, Henry had said, was simply excessive shyness. Alone with Vivien, he was probably quite different.

Over lunch, they kept being interrupted by telephone

calls. These were mainly from members of the Costume
Society and other friends, whom Minna Maskell had lost
no time in telling of the Findons' troubles. Christine answered most of the calls, while Henry and Vivien between
them gave Barry a blow by blow account of the events of
the last twenty-four hours. Barry gazed at Vivien, mur-
muring what an abomination it all was, how the rise in
crime in the country was really terrifying, and how, if it
went on, a stage might be reached when each man might
begin to suspect his neighbour.

"No, no, I'm not joking, Henry," he went on earnestly.
"If you don't suspect your neighbour, perhaps you suspect
his teen-age sons and daughters. It's fantastic, the kind of
people who become involved in these outrages nowadays.
Just read your newspaper. The so-called educated are as
bad as everyone else. Drugs, sex, violence. It's happening
all over the world. No regard for human life or property or
freedom, unless perhaps your own, and you'll fight to protect that with clubs and knives, instead of trusting in the
law. It's all unspeakably degrading."

Irrationally, although she agreed with him, Christine
wanted to dispute this. Barry always had the effect on her
of making her want to contradict him. It was mainly because
she wanted to break through his concentration on Vivien,
to interrupt what felt almost like a private conversation going
on between the two of them.

She was just about to say that that sort of talk exaggerated
everything absurdly, when Vivien remarked, "In this house
you don't have to worry about teen-agers, but young David
here, aged nine, has already committed theft and arson."

She spoke cheerfully, as if by now she thought this rather
a good joke.

To Christine's surprise, David only gave her one swift
glance, then stared down at his plate. There was no explosion. Frances was equally subdued. It looked as if they had
taken to heart the warning that they should be careful how
they talked, and had agreed between themselves not to talk
at all. But there was a sullen and scornful set to David's
lips and there had been burning rage in the glance that he
had given Vivien.

Simon came to his defence. "You've no proof at all he took those shoes, Vivien. Personally, I don't think he did."

"Ah, let's not get started on that," she said. "Forget the shoes. I didn't mean to drag them in. They're so unimportant compared with everything else that's happened. And I expect I did just as insufferable things when I was his age."

"But you're still sure he took them," Simon went on.

Before she could reply, Barry resumed his private conversation with her. "But of course, of course it's unimportant. A complete red herring. And I've brought some other shoes for you. I do hope I've picked out the right ones. Just a pair of walking shoes and some bedroom slippers. That's what you said you wanted, wasn't it? Perhaps we could go for a walk this afternoon. Drive out of the town a little way and stretch our legs. That would do you good, I expect. Calm your nerves and make you sleep well tonight."

"Talking of shoes—" Henry said.

"Must we?" Vivien said sharply.

"Oh, these are the other ones I was going to talk about," Henry said. "The antique ones. That green silk shoe that David helped himself to this morning has a silver buckle on it, hasn't it? And you'd some other buckles on show at the dinner last night. Paste, you said. Well, are any of those buckles by any chance of any value?"

"No," Vivien answered. "The best one's worth perhaps ten pounds. The others are nearer the four- or five-pound level. I told you the collection isn't valuable, didn't I? What made you think of the buckles?"

"I was just trying to account for Lew's behaviour this morning," Henry said. Lew was not with them. He had refused to join them for lunch, taking some bread and cheese up to his room instead. "He saw that silver buckle on the green shoe and I simply wondered if it had suggested something to him. I don't know what. But I've been puzzling over that little scene he made ever since it happened."

"Always remembering," Simon said, "that Lew might be rather inclined to make a scene for the sake of making a scene."

"I don't know," Henry said doubtfully. "I've a

feeling...Well, it doesn't matter. I suppose he could be acting strangely, just from shock."

"On top of which, he's frightened," Vivien said. "That's the impression that scene gave me, anyway."

But perhaps, Christine thought, they were all more frightened than they wanted to admit. Officially they all subscribed to the belief in the burglar, the man who had come in from outside, and been caught by Mrs. Heacham in the storeroom while Marsha, Lew, and Roddie were out. But what Barry had said about reaching a state where every man suspected his neighbour was uncomfortably near the bone. For one thing, there was the problem of why nothing had been stolen. So they were beginning to slip, half-unconsciously, into a mood of distrusting one another, of watching slight changes of expression on each other's faces and pondering what they could signify, of listening for double meanings in what was said. The air of normality after which they were all striving was false. They were a group of tense and anxious people.

After lunch Vivien and Barry left for the Crown, taking Vivien's two suitcases with them. Then Marsha suggested that she should take David and Frances to the cinema, as there was a film on about wild animals in Africa which the children might like, and Simon said that wild animals in Africa were something about which he had always felt that he had never known enough and that he would like to join the party. They all went off together, leaving the house to Henry and Christine and the lonely Lew upstairs.

She was worried about Lew. She said to Henry that it seemed to her that there was something callous about leaving him to himself in this way, and Henry looked worried too, but said that with Lew's unfortunate childhood, it probably came naturally to him to hide his feelings in his attic, rather than to show any need for sympathy. So Christine stacked the dishwasher with all the dishes that they had used at lunch, made some fresh coffee and settled down to drink it with Henry in the sitting room.

For a little while they felt relaxed and peaceful. The house was quiet. Very few sounds reached them from the street. The telephone had stopped ringing. They sat side by side on the sofa, Christine with her feet drawn up under her, Henry with his arm round her shoulders. Her head rested on his shoulder and her eyelids began to feel very heavy.

Then Mrs. Heacham came in. Just as she had when Christine had been making the salad in the kitchen, she seemed to come and stand over them, watching them with that resentful gaze which she had always been able to make them feel even through several closed doors. She had been resentful of them in life because of all that they had that fate, or her own nature, had denied her. If she had been alive now, she would have resented these few moments of peace, would have interrupted them, if she could have thought of an excuse for doing so, would have struggled to destroy their dependence on one another...

Christine sat up with a start.

"Henry, do you think this house is going to be haunted?" she asked.

He patted her head back to where it had been a moment before.

"No," he said.

"Well, I'm being haunted," she said. "Mrs. Heacham is after me."

"She'll be after us both till we find out what really happened here yesterday," he answered.

"The destroyer destroyed."

"What?"

"She was a destroyer," Christine said. "The only strong feelings she ever had were destructive. Envy, resentment, possessiveness. She's blighted us ever since she came to live here."

Henry seemed surprised that she felt so strongly about it. "I always thought she was a pathetic old thing."

"Pathos was the main weapon in her armoury. That dignified independence of hers that clutched at your heart. But never leaving you in peace. Always making you feel unrighteously fortunate."

"Yes, I know, but actually the only harm she ever did was to Lew. She made rather a mess of him, I agree."

"She'd begun to do me harm," Christine said, "and the proof of it is the way I feel now that she's trailing me about the house, making some horrible demand on me. I do hope I'm not going to start getting a thing about this house—you know, that I'll never be free of her till we leave it. I don't want to leave it. I love it."

"Of course you do," Henry said. "So do I. And I tell you what, Christine, I think I'll really get down to the garden soon, start digging up some of that lawn, lay it out quite differently, make it interesting. If I got on with the digging this winter, we could really start operations in the spring. We've often talked about having peaches against that south wall, and we could order some shrubs, not the commonplace ones that everyone has, but something a bit unusual. Where are those catalogues? Let's start making a list. And I really will get ahead with the job this year."

Christine went to the bureau and burrowed in one of the drawers for the garden catalogues that various nurserymen had sent them from time to time. Sitting on the hearth rug, the two of them drank coffee, and Henry read out the names of shrubs and Christine agreed or disagreed with him as to their suitability for their garden, both of them playing a game of pretence that would have put any game of David's into the shade. It was a game that they often tended to play when something was wrong which they did not want to think about. The fact that Henry was determined to plan the garden now meant that he was having almost as much trouble as Christine in keeping Mrs. Heacham's ghost at bay.

They had just decided that they must have a *prunus subhertila autumnalis*, that lovely, delicate, winter flowering cherry, when Henry abruptly tossed the catalogue and pencil aside. He stretched his legs out across the hearth rug, leant back against the sofa and folded his hands behind his head.

"This isn't any good, our minds aren't on it," he said. "Christine, I've had an idea nagging at the back of my mind all day, and I haven't wanted to talk about it because it's about Lew, and I've got that guilty sort of feeling you know about that Lew's never had a chance and that there's something peculiarly brutal about blackening his character. But this is just between you and me and nobody else need know about it, need they?"

She nodded.

"Well, listen," Henry said. "Suppose the main thing in this affair is that it's a crime that didn't come off. Suppose it was meant to be quite different. Suppose someone came here to steal the snuffboxes—"

"But—"

"Wait. Someone, with Lew to help him, was going to take the snuffboxes last night when we were all out. I don't know how they knew we were going to be out, but somehow they found out, and Lew came here, apparently to make peace with his mother, the night before. And suppose Lew's part of the job was simply to undo the lock and bolts on the back door and clear out to the Bull and get himself an alibi. Then his friend would have come in, helped himself to the snuffboxes, or anyway, the best ones, and disappeared. But there turned out to be complications. First of all, there were Roddie and Marsha here. So Lew had to get them to go out with him. He managed that all right and left the back door unlocked as arranged. But then Mrs. Heacham, who hadn't had her supper as usual, because she wanted to have it with Lew, came down looking for him and walked slap into his friend. And the friend lost his head and killed her. Perhaps he didn't mean to. Perhaps he just meant to knock her out and bolt. But she was old and frail, and she died. So he bundled her body into the trunk and made off as fast as he could."

"Without the snuffboxes."

"Yes, without the snuffboxes—because what had been meant to be a fairly minor crime had turned into a very serious one, not just theft, but murder, and if any of those snuffboxes had got into the hands of a fence, he'd probably have been afraid to handle them. He might even have turned in the people who offered them, for his own protection. And Lew would have come back and found the snuffboxes were still there and wouldn't have known what had gone wrong, because he wouldn't have found his mother's body, but naturally he wouldn't have given anything away. And then her body was found this morning and he's understood what happened. And he's blaming himself hideously, because he isn't a violent type, but he daren't say anything about the other fellow, because it would involve him in the

crime. So he's getting more and more desperate, not knowing what to do—and what he *will* do is something I'm rather
worried about."

"But when he shouted at David that he'd told him everything, what did he mean?" Christine asked.

"I think it was the snuffbox in David's hand that made
him say it," Henry answered. "At first I thought about the
buckle on the shoe. I thought if the buckles were valuable,
it might be those that he and his friend had come after.
Suppose Lew mixes in crooked circles in London, I thought,
he might somehow have got word that that part of the collection was going to be here for the night, and so he came
here just at this time to see his mother. And when he saw
David wearing that shoe, he thought it was David's way of
saying that he understood about the buckles. After all, the
children were here in the house last night. Lew can't know
what they may have seen and understood."

"I don't believe they saw anything or understand anything," Christine said.

"No, but how's Lew to be sure of that? However, it seems
I was wrong about the buckles. Vivien says they aren't of
any value. So that leaves the snuffboxes, which would be
easy to pocket, probably easy to dispose of, and a few of
them are sufficiently valuable to be worth taking. If Lew
saw David flourishing that snuffbox at him and thought he
was being threatened—"

The front doorbell rang.

"Not visitors!" Christine groaned.

"More likely the police back again," Henry said, "or even
the press."

They both got to their feet and went to the door together.

It was the police. A sergeant and a constable were on the
doorstep, with a police car in the street behind them.

"I'm sorry to trouble you again, Mr. Findon," the sergeant
said, "but we've come to the conclusion we'd like to ask
Mr. Louis Heacham a few more questions, and it would
probably be easiest for everyone if he came to the police
station with us."

"I see," Henry said. "Well, he's up in his room. I'll fetch
him."

"Don't trouble, we can do it," the sergeant said. "I remember the way."

He and the constable made for the stairs.

Henry and Christine exchanged glances and, without speaking, decided together to follow them.

Lew was not in his room. Nor were any possessions that he might have brought with him. He was not anywhere else in the house either. Lew had gone.

So had the gold snuffbox with the ruby monogram on it, as well as the three other most valuable snuffboxes in the corner cabinet.

# 8

As soon as they were sure that Lew was missing, the two policemen went away again. Henry asked them why they wanted Lew, but they hedged, indicating that it was not for them to say. About an hour later Mr. Ditteridge reappeared, seemed to be pleased to find only Henry and Christine at home and said that he would like a talk with them. They took him into the sitting room, where he sat down, gave a long sigh, and as if the thought of what he had to talk about only oppressed him and he would far sooner have talked of something else, remarked, "This is a nice room."

"It is, isn't it?" Henry agreed.

"And that's a nice bit of garden. But you haven't a dog, have you? With a garden like that you could easily keep a dog. Just put a bit of fence across from the garage to the wall and he'd be safe from traffic, yet he wouldn't be confined."

"We've sometimes thought of it," Henry said, "but somehow we've never got around to it."

"We've a dog," Mr. Ditteridge said, "but living in a flat it's sometimes quite a problem. The wife and I would like to move to a house where he'd have a bit more freedom— we've got our name down for one—but it isn't all that easy to get."

"That's a pity."

"Yes, he'd be much better off with a garden. But there you are, you can't have everything." Mr. Ditteridge sighed again and said, "Mr. Findon, how much do you and Mrs. Findon know about Lew Heacham?"

"Not very much," Henry said. "Just what I told you yesterday, that he grew up in my father's home, then when he was seventeen ran away and we never heard anything about him until yesterday morning, when he told us he'd come because he wanted to make peace with his mother."

"You didn't know, for instance, that he'd got a record."

"A police record?"

"Yes, he's been in gaol for demanding money with menaces. As a matter of fact, he's wanted for that now. If he turned up here suddenly, without any warning, I think it could have been because he thought it was a convenient place to hide out."

"Somehow that doesn't altogether surprise me," Henry said.

"You were suspicious of him?"

"I wouldn't go as far as that. I didn't want to be suspicious of him. I'd always felt he'd had a pretty grim sort of childhood, and that that was partly my family's fault, even if it was mostly his mother's, and I hoped there'd be a chance to help him somehow. Certainly we were ready to let him stay here for a while. All the same, there was something about him that didn't ring true."

Mr. Ditteridge looked at Christine. "Is that how you felt too, Mrs. Findon?"

"More or less," she said.

"How do you think his mother felt about him? Did she know the truth?"

"She was uneasy about him," Christine said. "She said he was no good. She also said that if he got into trouble, she wasn't going to lift a finger to help him. She was very bitter because he'd run away from her when she'd worked so hard for him. She also said that he hadn't even known she was home from Canada, and that he'd only come to see what he could get out of us, and that when he saw her, he looked as if he'd like to turn tail and run away. I don't know if that was true. Lew himself said he'd written to her sister in Canada and found out where she was living and had come to see her. But Mrs. Heacham herself didn't believe that, and said she was only doing her best to warn us."

"If she'd known the true story of how he spent the last few years, do you think she'd have turned him in to us?" Mr. Ditteridge asked.

"I doubt it," Christine said. "I don't think she'd have wanted to face the shame of it herself. I remember she said to me that that sort of shame was something she'd been spared."

"How did he spend the last few years?" Henry asked.

"Mainly as chauffeur or manservant to wealthy people," Mr. Ditteridge answered, "doing the job very well, getting their confidence, then disappearing with some letters or other confidential papers and holding them up to ransom. He was clever about it too, not going too far, and good at picking the sort of victims who wouldn't inform against him. We knew about him, of course, long before we were able to nail him, but at last he blundered, threatening to expose a man to his wife when he'd only been waiting hopefully for her to divorce him. So we got Heacham that time, though he didn't get much of a sentence, as it was officially a first offence. But it got his pictures in the papers, and if his mother sometimes got English papers in Canada, perhaps she saw it and so knew all about it when he turned up here. And that could have given him a motive for murdering her. After all, it looks as if she might have been killed because she knew too much about someone. I mean, since it doesn't look as if she obstructed anyone in committing any other crime, like stealing something, for instance."

"I've a theory about that," Henry said. "Just an idea. But perhaps I should tell you."

He went on to tell Mr. Ditteridge his idea about the crime that hadn't happened the evening before, the theft of the snuffboxes.

Mr. Ditteridge thought it over with a good deal of seriousness before he commented, "It's a theory. Interesting. I must bear it in mind."

"You don't think much of it," Henry said.

Mr. Ditteridge wrinkled his high, narrow forehead. "Oh, I wouldn't say that. If Heacham had picked up with someone else, as you suggest, if all he had to do was make sure a door was left open and everyone was out of the way, and if his mother's death was really as much of a shock to him as it seemed to be, well, that's certainly worth thinking about. But in the past he seems to have worked alone and been very cagey about whom he took up with. Still, it's worth thinking about. If you have any more ideas about it, please let me know. I'll be grateful."

He stood up, repeated that he was grateful for their co-operation, and left them. Christine looked at the clock and decided that it was time to go to the kitchen to review what they could have for dinner that evening.

Much as she had often wanted the freedom of her own kitchen during the past months, she was in no mood to bother much with cooking now. She decided on soup, which she could make by putting the bone from the sirloin to simmer with a variety of chopped vegetables, to be followed by spaghetti with a jar of bottled meat sauce. Then the family could have more salad and more cheese, if they wanted it. It was going to take her some days, she realised, to get the feeling of things again.

She was in the middle of chopping up the vegetables for the soup when Marsha came in and asked if she could help. She, Simon, David, and Frances had just returned from the cinema, and the children came rushing into the kitchen after her, back to their normal cheerfulness. The film had been super, anyway, the animals had been super, the lions and the elephants and the rhinoceroses and the crocodiles. But there had been some romance in the film, which they had thought poor stuff. Then they said that they were hungry and would like some orange squash and some anchovies on toast.

Christine had never wanted things like anchovies on toast when she was their age, but she abandoned the vegetables to open a tin of anchovies and make the toast. When David and Frances were given these, they went off with them to the sitting room to tell Henry in minutest detail the story of the film from start to finish. Marsha, meanwhile, had got to work on the vegetables.

"Where's Lew?" she asked.

"Gone," Christine said.

Marsha looked round, startled. "Gone?"

"Cleared out some time in the afternoon with some of our snuffboxes," Christine said, "and just in time, from his own point of view, because the police came here, wanting him to help them in their inquiries."

Marsha gave a little cry. "They're going to arrest him?"

"They've got to find him first."

"But he didn't kill his mother! I'm absolutely sure he didn't!"

"I'm not sure it's for that they want him," Christine said. "They've got other things against him. It seems he's given to demanding money with menaces, and had gone a bit too far for once, and may have come here to hide. And he's definitely a thief."

"But he didn't kill his mother!" Marsha repeated with soft intensity. "I know he didn't."

"Do you mean you actually know, or is it intuition?"

Marsha was slicing up a carrot. "You'd call it intuition, I expect. I call it knowing. I think you can simply know whether or not a person is capable of a thing like murder without all the circumstantial evidence stuff."

"Even if you only met him yesterday?"

Marsha gave a sigh and said, "Yesterday feels like years ago, doesn't it? I feel as if today has been going on forever. Yes—even if I only met him yesterday. Not with everybody, of course. Take Simon, now. I really don't understand him at all. He's too complicated. I can't make out which of his feelings are really him and which he's making up. But Lew's quite simple. He's no good at hiding things. Last night, for instance, all the evening, he was silly and cheerful and quite at ease. But all today he's been frightened. As soon as he discovered his mother had been killed, he got terrified. But if he'd killed her before we went out together yesterday, he'd have been terrified then."

"If he didn't kill her, what's he been so frightened of today?" Christine asked.

"I suppose he knew the police would soon find out about his record and would suspect him, just because of it."

"I expect you're right. Anyway, I expect the police will find him quite quickly."

The thought seemed to depress Marsha. She appeared to have taken quite a liking to Lew. She left Christine in the kitchen, and Christine heard her going upstairs, her feet dragging for once, as if she were thinking deeply.

Simon came in a few minutes later, bringing Christine a glass of sherry.

"I thought you might like this," he said, sitting down at the table. He had brought a drink for himself too. "Henry's listening patiently to the story of the film, putting on a pretty good show of being enthralled. Having actually seen it, I didn't see why I should suffer it all over again."

Christine took the sherry gratefully. "Has he told you about Lew?"

"That the police want him and that he's gone, yes. And Henry's own theory too, about someone coming here to get the snuffboxes last night, and giving up, after committing the murder. But if you don't mind, Christine, let's not talk about Lew or the murder."

She lifted the lid off the saucepan, saw that the soup was simmering, and sat down facing him at the table. She drank some sherry.

"What else is there to talk about?" she asked. "Henry and I spent the afternoon trying to talk about the garden, but it was very hard work."

"There's me," Simon said. "Me and Marsha. Christine, if I persuaded her to marry me, would I be bound to spoil her life?"

It took Christine by surprise. It was not like Simon to be thinking either of marriage or too much of what harm he might do another person.

"Why are you afraid you might?" she asked.

"I've spoilt so many things at different times of my life."

She thought that this was probably true, but that this was not the right time to agree with him.

"Marsha was in here just now," she said, "and she made

the startling statement that she didn't understand you. Have you said anything of this kind to her yet?"

"I haven't said a bloody thing to her. I mean that more or less literally. All the way home from the cinema, I couldn't think of a single thing to say. I walked along in a dead silence as if I'd never been so bored by anyone before. But it was because the only thing I could think of to say was would she marry me. But I knew in the present circumstances she'd say no."

"She's got a nice nature," Christine said. "She might just have said she'd think it over. She wouldn't want to hurt your feelings."

Simon's sombre face brightened for a moment. "That's what one feels about her straightaway, isn't it? I think I felt that about her even before I'd taken in how lovely she was." He put his elbows on the table, nursed his glass between his hands and gazed into it as if he were trying to read the future in a crystal. For once his rather hard grey eyes looked uncertain. He had lost the air of knowing just where he was going and what he was doing that usually made him slightly formidable. "I'm scared," he said at last. "I don't feel safe. I feel I'm on the edge of doing something wildly dangerous, particularly for her."

"I think she's actually very tough," Christine said. "She can look after herself."

"I hope so, because I've got the feeling that here's something I want very badly, and when that happens to me, I don't waste any more time than I can help."

"Well, I hope it goes as you want. I hope it works out," she said.

"Of course, if it does..." He paused, giving Christine a long look and a wry smile. "I might more or less lose you. I mean, it might be rather much to expect her to understand our relationship as Henry does."

She almost told him that Henry had not understood it as well as Simon and she had assumed. But that seemed in a fashion disloyal to Henry.

"I'll miss you," she said. "But you must have noticed at different times that I've worked quite hard at trying to get you married off."

132 Foot in the Grave

"That was just automatic," he said. "Normal female stuff. You never expected it to succeed."

"Anyway, I like Marsha a lot better than any of the others I can remember."

"Still, it would be nice if you could manage to feel just a pang of regret," he said. "Just a very small pang. Couldn't you do that?"

"Simon, dear, I'm feeling eaten up with jealousy," she answered, and it was not untrue. She had depended on him for so much and taken his curious kind of fidelity so for granted, that the thought of handing him over wholly to another woman felt unexpectedly painful.

Luckily he did not probe.

"I suppose she knows what's happened to me," he said.

"I shouldn't be surprised."

"Has she said anything about it to you?"

"Not directly."

"A girl like that will have had a certain amount of practice in noticing how men feel about her."

"Oh, for certain."

"She hasn't confided in you that she's in love with anyone else, has she?"

She shook her head.

"Splendid," he said. "But what nonsense I've been talking, haven't I? I wonder if I really mean any of it, or if it's just a way of getting my mind off murder. Thank you for letting me chat. Now I'll let you go on with your cooking, shall I?"

"Oh, for God's sake, Simon!" Christine exclaimed. "For once in your life don't run away from things! It's always the things you really want that you're careful not to go after, in case you don't get them. Stop being so chicken-hearted."

"Chicken-hearted? Me?" He looked genuinely startled.

"Always," she said. "I expect that's why you've become rich and successful, and those are very nice things to be, and if they're what you want most, don't worry, just stick to them. But if you want some of the other things, go after them, and don't worry too much either about how successful you're going to be."

"It's so easy to say that when you've got all you want," he said. "You and Henry..."

"Well, you've got charm and riches."

"And I don't want to be loved for either, thank you," he answered. "The riches I wouldn't much mind, but the charm would just show she was dim-witted, wouldn't it? It can be turned on or off like a tap, when one feels inclined. No, I'd like to be wanted for being intolerable, selfish, edgey, suspicious, as well as generally irrational."

"But that follows naturally. Not all at once. But step by step, it develops."

"As if you knew anything about it—"

He stopped as the doorbell rang.

Going to answer it, she reflected that most people they knew probably thought that neither Henry nor she had any knowledge of those deplorable human qualities to which Simon had just referred, whereas in fact they both had profound knowledge of all of them and the fact that they were not afraid of letting them show their ugly teeth from time to time was one of the satisfactions of their marriage. They could each be at their worst with one another, and yet feel safe.

But of course this had not come about quickly, or without pain. That was where Simon had gone wrong, wanting Marsha to love him already for the dark side of his pleasant nature. He wanted everything all at once.

Opening the front door, Christine found Rodney Maskell there, holding an enormous bunch of pink carnations.

She took for granted that the carnations were for Marsha, but it turned out that they were a present from his mother to Christine. To cheer her up, Rodney said. They had come from the Maskells' greenhouse, which was a vast place in which Tony Maskell, with great skill and dedication, kept an immense variety of plants flowering all the year round.

Christine took Rodney to the sitting room, then went to the kitchen to find a vase for the carnations. Simon was still sitting at the table, and hearing that Rodney had brought the flowers, sneered at them, saying that he detested carnations almost as much as orchids, and would never insult a woman by giving her any.

Christine said that what he needed was probably another drink and sent him off to the sitting room. Then taking a tall green glass jug out of a cupboard, she arranged the flowers in it, and followed him.

She found David and Frances sitting on the hearth rug, playing snakes-and-ladders. Rodney and Marsha were sitting side by side on the sofa, each with a glass of sherry. Henry had a gin and tonic in his hand, and Simon was just pouring one out for himself.

In his solemn, quiet voice, Rodney was saying, ". . . and as I may not be coming down next weekend, I thought I'd just like to say, I hope this thing gets sorted out quickly, so that you don't have a too awful time."

"Thank you, Rodney," Henry said. "We hope so too."

"But why aren't you coming down?" Christine asked. "You usually do."

"Well, I—you know how it is, things seem to have accumulated—work, I mean, and all that. Sometimes I bring work home with me, but I never seem to get any done, so I thought—well, perhaps for a weekend or two, I'll stay in London and try to catch up with things."

Christine knew that Marsha had only to say that she hoped that he would have caught up with things soon for him to say that perhaps he would come down next weekend after all, but Marsha was silent.

He lingered on for a few minutes, going into further complicated and unnecessary explanations of why he might not be visiting his parents for a few weeks, while Marsha remained silent, though a look of distress came into her eyes. She also grew fidgety, as if she could hardly contain her impatience for him to be gone. Perhaps he felt this himself, for suddenly he finished what was left of his sherry in one swallow, stood up clumsily and apologising deeply for the fact that he must leave so soon, said good-bye individually to each of them and at last left. Henry saw him to the door.

As soon as Rodney had gone, Marsha also finished her sherry at a gulp, grabbed each of the children by an arm, hauled them to their feet and said, "Come on, it's time for your baths."

"It isn't!" David cried. He had just thrown the dice and what had come up would just take him safely past the head of a very long, threatening snake. "It's much too early."

"Come along, don't argue!" Marsha said with unusual fierceness.

Hearing that unfamiliar ring in her voice, the children meekly went with her. She had gone a little pale and looked distraught. It had upset her to hurt Rodney.

With both her and Rodney out of the room, Simon relaxed, lying back in his chair, stretching his legs out comfortably and smiling at Christine.

"Don't look so smug!" she snapped. She had not enjoyed watching Rodney suffer either. "It could be you next time."

"Then I'll know what to expect," he said. "I'll know that she minds, and isn't just doing it for pleasure. That'll help. I may be able to exploit the knowledge." He looked up at Henry as he came back into the room. "Henry, has it struck you that that young man happens to have no alibi for yesterday evening?"

"Rodney?" Henry said and laughed. "He's the kind of person who'd never need one."

"What makes you think that?" Simon seemed to be serious.

Henry recognised it and said uneasily, "We've known him half his life. I taught him at Colnehill. His work was a little lacking in imagination, but it was good sound plodding stuff. And a good sound plodding type is what he is. Don't let your own imagination run away with you."

"If you knew how many crooks I've met who appear to be good sound plodding citizens," Simon said.

"Have you known a lot of crooks, Simon?" Christine asked, interested. "You've never mentioned it before."

"That was just a manner of speaking," he answered, "though in my kind of work, you meet all kinds. All the get-rich-quick people. And sometimes you can't help wondering how the bit of capital that they're starting out with came to stick to their fingers."

"That isn't the same thing as murder," Henry said.

"But according to your own theory," Simon went on, "the murder wasn't meant to happen. The crime that was

meant to happen, and didn't then, was the theft of the
snuffboxes. So suppose Rodney and Lew in fact knew each
other quite well up in London. Finding they both had a kind
of connection with you might have helped to get that going.
And suppose Rodney told Lew how you'd got a collection
of snuffboxes and Lew remembered that collection and knew
it was quite valuable, and Rodney told Lew how you and
Christine were going to be out yesterday evening, and how
it would be easy to get Marsha out of the house too, and
how, while she and Lew were in the Bull, Rodney could
slip into the house again by the back door, if Lew left it
unlocked for him, and take the collection. As the sort of
man you all think he is, Rodney was never going to be
suspected, and it was unlikely anyone would notice the fact
that while the other two were in the pub, Rodney was on
his own. But of course it all went wrong because Mrs.
Heacham caught him as he came in, and he lost his head
and killed her, then hadn't the nerve to go ahead with the
theft."

There was a moment of silence, then Henry said to Christine, "You know, he's serious."

"He's serious because he's jealous," she said. "Isn't that
the reason, Simon?"

"No," he answered. "Perhaps it's why I like my theory,
but it isn't what made me think of it. I thought of it because
it fits the facts."

"But the Maskells are loaded with money," Henry said,
"and they don't keep Rodney short."

"Suppose he's got into trouble of some kind, gambling
or something, that he doesn't want to tell them about."

"But Lew's accomplice could have been anyone. Any
member of the crowd he goes with in London."

"Only how did he know you'd got the snuffboxes?" Simon
asked. "He might have seen the notice of Father's death in
the *Times*, but for all he knew, that collection might have
been left to me, not you, or even sold. So if you're right
that the motive behind the crime was the theft of it, then
he must have had contact fairly recently with someone who
told him you'd got it, and where it was, and what the set-

up was in the house. Of course, that could have been Mrs. Heacham herself, but if she was in on the business, why should she have been killed for walking in on it?"

"Is that your only reason for thinking she wasn't in on it?" Henry asked. "You don't think it's unlikely simply because we happen to have known her for years, and she's always been dead honest and reliable? That doesn't weigh with you."

"I'm just trying to look at the facts with as much detachment as possible," Simon said. "Of course, one can't help letting them be coloured to some extent by one's personal feelings."

"In the end, however, you don't really trust anybody," Henry said.

"Good lord, I trust people all the time," Simon said. "Much more than you do. And with thousands of pounds. The financial world couldn't work at all without trust all round."

"Isn't that a case of taking calculated risks, rather than trusting people?" Henry went on.

"Well, perhaps," Simon agreed.

"Let me point out then," Henry said, "that if one looks at these facts you've been mentioning with real detachment, and without letting one's view of them be coloured by one's personal feelings, one could come up with the idea that you were Lew's accomplice. Had you thought of that?"

Simon grinned. "Actually, I had," he said, "and I was wondering when you were going to get around to it. I might easily have a motive. It could be that I've always coveted the snuffboxes. True, Father's glass and silver came to me, but perhaps the snuffboxes were what I'd always wanted. Or perhaps my finances have been doing badly lately, and I'm desperate for a few thousand pounds. And perhaps the truth is that Lew and I have been seeing each other off and on for years, and he got everyone out of the house and left the back door unlocked for me. And I came down by train and taxi instead of by car because I didn't want my car to be recognised. It's quite a case you can make out against me. But there are one or two big holes in it."

Henry turned to Christine. He was looking intrigued. "Do you know, he's really given this matter some serious thought. What are the holes, Simon?"

"The main one is simply that if Mrs. Heacham caught me in the storeroom, I'd have had no need to kill her," Simon replied. "I could just have said, 'Oh, hallo, Mrs. Heacham, how nice to see you. How are you?' And if she'd asked me how I'd got in, I could swear I'd found the front door ajar. And if she'd asked what I was doing in the storeroom, I could have said I thought I'd heard a noise there. And the theft of the snuffboxes could have waited for another opportunity. Apart from that, it would have been rather a bad mistake to take a taxi right to the door, then when no one came to open it, getting him to take me to the Crown for dinner, then taking another taxi back *before you and Christine got back from your dinner*. If I'd been carefully setting up an alibi, I'd have come and gone inconspicuously, never gone to the Crown at all, and arrived here after you'd got home, saying I'd come on the late train. Then I seem to remember that I'm the person who drew your attention to the fact that the snuffboxes might be missing. Do you think I'd have done that if I'd meant to steal them, but had inadvertently committed a murder instead?"

Henry laughed. "All right, you don't make as good a suspect as I thought. But I can offer you a better one. Marsha."

The smile faded from Simon's face. His hand tightened on the glass that he was holding.

"Oh yes," he said. "I've given that some thought also. She rather likes Lew, doesn't she? She probably likes him a lot better than Rodney. And that just possibly might be because she's known him a lot longer than we think. And if she has, she could be the one who told Lew about the snuffboxes being here, and who got him to come here when you were all going to be out. And she definitely is the one who got Lew and Rodney out of the house, then she and Lew went and set up a noticeable alibi in the Bull, to which she didn't fail to draw your attention. She could have wanted you to realise that an intruder could have got in while they were out. And if Mrs. Heacham interrupted them after they'd got back, just as they were actually helping themselves to the snuffboxes, they might have chased her out to the storeroom and killed her."

The smile on Henry's face was a bit lopsided now.

"You've fallen in love with the girl, haven't you, Simon?"

"It would seem so," Simon replied gravely. "It's my present assessment of the situation."

"Yet you don't trust her an inch. I was right when I said you don't trust anybody."

"Didn't you say also I take calculated risks? If falling in love isn't a calculated risk . . ."

"Uncalculated, usually."

"Oh no, because even now I could run for it. But I'm wantonly exposing myself to further danger. And as it happens, I know that everything I've just said about Marsha is completely untrue, for the simple reason that I feel it in my bones. Isn't that trust?"

Christine stood up.

"You've both been talking a lot of nonsense," she said. "Marsha, Rodney, Simon—all such likely murderers. What about Vivien and Barry? I know that Vivien was at the dinner and Barry was in London, but you shouldn't forget them. And Minna and Tony Maskell were here in the house for a little while, and might have done a hurried murder while they were washing their hands. And when is one of you going to suggest that I killed Mrs. Heacham? Now I'm going to take a look at the soup, and I think we'll eat in the kitchen."

# 9

They all went to bed early. Christine was so tired, in a tense
and nervous way which made her think that a sleeping pill
might be a good idea, that when Henry and she went into
their bedroom and she realised that she had never finished
tidying it up, she felt complete indifference. Let everything
stay just where it was until tomorrow, she thought. Then
she noticed the shirt that Henry had worn at the dinner. She
picked it up and showed him the cuff with the red-brown
smear on it.

"Is that blood or isn't it?" she asked.

"Looks like it," he said.

"Did you prick or scratch yourself yesterday?"

"Not that I noticed." He looked at his wrist, then held
it out for her to inspect.

"I can't see anything," she said.

They were both silent. Neither of them wanted to talk or
even to think about what that red-brown smear could mean.

Dropping the shirt back on the chair from which she had
picked it up, Christine began to undress. She took a sleeping
pill and suggested to Henry that he should do the same, but
he shook his head and said that his problem for the last hour
or two had been to keep awake at all. But of course that
did not mean that as soon as they were in bed and the light
was out their eyes would not open and both of them stare
wakefully at the darkness.

After they had lain there for a little while, each knowing from the small movements of the other that they were both awake, Henry said, "If that *is* blood on that shirt, Christine, you know when it got there."

"Yes, when you went into the storeroom to fetch the cane for Vivien."

"When did you realise that?"

"I'm not sure. Some time ago. Perhaps when I first found it. But there seemed to be so much else to think about."

"You see what it means, don't you?"

"Yes, that Mrs. Heacham was killed before we ever left the house."

"Yes, and I suppose it was about half-past six when I went into the storeroom for the cane. And I must have brushed my wrist against the handle of the trunk Mrs. Heacham was in when I was reaching for the cane behind it. That's where it was, you know—in that corner behind the trunk."

"Does it make any difference?" Christine asked. "It just means Lew let someone into the house rather earlier than we thought he did."

"If it was Lew."

"Don't you think it must have been?"

"I suppose so. I don't know. I've had some fairly weird ideas. I've even wondered, for instance, if Simon's idea that Mrs. Heacham let the murderer in mightn't be right. Not for theft, of course. But I think how we've always taken for granted that her husband was dead, as she told us. But suppose he wasn't. Suppose he's been doing a long sentence in gaol, and just got out, and Lew came here to warn her, because she'd given the man away in the first place, and he might be after revenge. Or he might have been in and out of gaol several times during the last fifteen years, and lived off her in betweenwhiles. That might have been why she went to Canada."

"And he tracked her down here, and came here tonight and she finally refused to help him, so he lost his temper and killed her."

"Is that so farfetched? Then there's another idea I had."

Christine wished that he would stop having ideas. The

pill was beginning to take hold and she wanted to let herself sink into the comforting depths of sleep.

"Mmm?" she said.

"I've wondered if it was actually David who let the murderer into the house."

"David?" she echoed drowsily.

"Yes, if he'd made friends with someone he met in the town, someone who persuaded him what a good joke it would be to let him into the house secretly."

"Why?"

"Well, there's always something about a secret when you're that age, isn't there? Just for its own sake. And I've a feeling, if that's what happened, it could somehow explain the theft of Vivien's shoes. We've been rather forgetting about those, haven't we?"

"How would it explain that?"

"Well, if it was the snuffboxes the man was after, he'd have had to get David out of the way, wouldn't he, while he grabbed them? So he might have given David some sort of fantastic job to do, like stealing somebody's left shoes—making it the left shoes just to make it more difficult and keep him busy a little longer. It would all have been just a great joke. And perhaps they didn't have to be Vivien's, they could just as well have been yours or Marsha's, only David happened to have taken a dislike to Vivien..."

At what point Henry's quiet speech faded from Christine's consciousness she could not remember later, but at some point it became mixed up in a dream in which she seemed to be at a funeral, which was also an inquest, and in which a gravestone was erected straightaway above the open grave, whose it was she did not know, and on the gravestone were carved the words, *Cause of death—Nemesis.*

Then the next thing that she was aware of was someone pounding on the door of the bedroom and a voice calling out, "Mrs. Findon! Mrs. Findon! Are David and Frances in there with you?"

As Christine sat up, trying to clear her head of the effects of the drug, she realised that the voice was Marsha's. Henry was already out of bed, wrapping his dressing gown round him. It was daylight. He opened the door. Marsha was on the landing, also in her dressing gown, with her thick fair hair hanging in an untidy mass around her shoulders. Her face was pale and scared. She looked past Henry into the room and saw that there was no one there but Christine.

"Oh God," she said, "then they've gone, they've really gone!"

Her loud knocking on the door and her excited voice had brought Simon out of his room too, the room that had been Vivien's the night before. He wanted to know what had happened.

"It's David and Frances," Marsha cried. "They aren't in their room, they aren't downstairs, they aren't in the garden—I've been out and looked. And their clothes are gone too, the ones they had on yesterday. They've got up and dressed and gone."

Christine was in her dressing gown too by then, and following Henry up the stairs to the children's bedroom.

The beds appeared to have been slept in, but when she felt them they were cold. So it was some time since the children had got up. The clothes that they had worn yesterday, as Marsha had said, were gone. So were their overcoats and the little white plastic handbag of which Frances was very proud, and which she always insisted on carrying with her when she went into the town, like a grown-up lady. At a quick glance Christine could not tell what else was missing, but when a thorough search had been made of the house, the garden and garage, there was no question of it. Like Lew, the children had gone.

The time was a little after 8:30.

The first thing that Henry did, once they were sure that the children were missing, was to telephone the police. After that he took the train and bus timetables out of a drawer in the bureau in the sitting room, and started searching through them for the London trains and buses.

"Why London, specially?" Simon asked.

"It's where their home is, isn't it?" Henry said. "They may even have a key to the flat. If they just felt they couldn't stand what was happening here any more, it might be where they'd make for."

They all seemed to arrive at the same conclusion then,

that it would be a good thing to get dressed, went to their rooms and hurried into clothes.

When Christine came down she was remembering that when she had drifted off to sleep, Henry had been talking about David letting a stranger into the house, and also of his taking Vivien's shoes. But she could not recall just what Henry had said, and the mention of Lew made her wonder if he had somehow kidnapped the children, had come into the house during the night and persuaded them to leave quietly with him. Of course, with no Mrs. Heacham to go the round of the house, no one had thought of fastening the chain on the front door, or the bolts on the back door. If Lew had acquired a key from his mother, he could easily have slipped in while everyone was asleep. Or he might have arranged with the children, before he left, that they should join him in the morning.

She felt a horrible chill go through her body as these thoughts passed through her mind. She began by keeping her fears to herself, but then she grabbed Henry's arm, drew him into the kitchen, where she had started to make tea, and told him what she had been thinking.

He put an arm round her and held her close.

"I know, I know!" he said. "Damn the brats, I expect they've just wandered off on their own, for God knows what crazy reason, but one can't help having these nightmares."

"You'd thought of it, then?" she asked.

"The moment I heard they were missing."

She took hold of the lapels of his jacket and hid her face against him.

"We'll find them, won't we?" she said. "Lew hasn't really done this. He isn't a monster."

"We don't know what he is," Henry muttered, "that's the trouble."

"If he wants a ransom, he can have everything we've got," she said. "But we haven't got so very much, and he must know that."

"It might sound a good deal to him."

He drew a deep, shaky breath. Christine let him go, stood back from him and looked up into his face. After a moment he knocked his forehead with his knuckles.

"Let's stop this," he said. "We're losing our heads, and that isn't doing the children or us any good. The police can check the trains and buses, and if David and Frances don't simply walk in for breakfast any time now, there are a lot of other things that can be done. Let's have that tea."

He went to get the tea and the teapot from the cupboard as the kettle came to the boil.

But David and Frances did not walk in for breakfast. Only the police arrived just as Henry was pouring the boiling water into the teapot, the same sergeant who had come the day before, accompanied by Joe Deeping. Joe was in uniform this morning and had some kind of little radio attached to his chest which talked steadily on and on all the time that he was in the house. For a moment, hearing that voice coming out of his chest and seeing his motionless lips, Christine thought that he was conducting a ventriloquial conversation with the sergeant, for reasons best known to themselves. But when Joe spoke to her, the quiet little cackle of speech went on without interruption.

He was noticeably upset, in spite of his stolidity, because he knew the children quite well and had taken a fancy to them.

"Linda'll be upset too," he said. "She'll be along soon, with Maureen, and Maureen always looks forward to coming and having a game with your little girl. But don't worry, Mrs. Findon, we'll soon find them for you. If they've wandered off on their own, they can't have got far."

"And if it wasn't on their own?" she said.

He was silent and left it to the sergeant to answer.

The sergeant asked her and Henry a number of questions, mostly about whether or not the children were likely to have made friends with any stranger without letting them know, and then about Lew and his relationship with them. Then he and Joe left. Just before they went, Henry remembered to tell them about the smear of blood on his cuff, and they took the shirt away with them. The tea had got cold, so Christine made a fresh pot, and made some toast and dumped it with butter, marmalade and milk on the kitchen table and left it for the others to help themselves. The housekeeping, which she had been nostalgically yearning to do for the last few months, was starting badly. But she would have to give it some thought later in the day. Supplies were running low. Of course, she could feed the family all day on eggs and open a few tins and telephone round the local shops, most of which still delivered to the house. But thinking about the matter at all felt appallingly difficult.

It was not only that she was out of practice and that when she sat down by the telephone to make a list of what was needed her thoughts moved from item to item as creakily and painfully as muscles that had not been used for a long time, but that a vision of David and Frances going off cheerfully and trustfully with Lew Heacham to God knew what destination, was printed so clearly on her mind that it blotted out everything else. At last she dialled the butcher and asked him to send up ten loin chops. Then she suddenly thought, "What am I going to do with ten loin chops if David and Frances don't come back?" So she changed the order to eight, then hurriedly changed it back to ten, because of course they would come back, of course...

She put the telephone down. She realised that she was beginning to get lightheaded. She had better sit still quietly for a few minutes, till she had control of herself. Then she would ask Marsha to go out and do the shopping for her.

She could not possibly leave the house herself, and she did not even like to go on using the telephone for long, in case the police tried to ring up with news, or Lew himself, or his accomplice, rang up with his ransom demand. Not that it would be as simple as that. There would be complicated instructions. They would be told to go to a telephone box, where they would find a note, or something like that, and the note would tell them what to do next. And the voice on the telephone, or the note, would tell them above all not to contact the police, because if they did that they would never see the children alive again...

They had never thought of that. They had contacted the police straightaway. Beginning to shiver, she sat staring at the telephone as if it had suddenly turned into a bomb that might explode in her face at any moment, yet from which it was impossible to tear herself away.

Henry came in to use it then, to ring up his headmaster

and explain something of the circumstances and to say that he hoped it would be all right if he stayed away from the school for the day. Christine left him in the middle of it and went back to the kitchen. A few minutes later Linda Deeping arrived.

She had not brought Maureen. Linda said that Joe had telephoned, telling her what had happened, and that she had thought that they would not want Maureen under their feet that morning, so she had asked Mrs. Ditteridge if she would take care of her.

"She was very nice about it," she said. "She said, 'Yes, Maureen and Pippy like each other, she's the one person Pippy never snaps at, so they can amuse themselves together while I see to the washing.' She also said, 'Please tell Mr. and Mrs. Findon how sorry I am for them.' She's very nice, Mrs. Ditteridge. I don't know how it is, I can never forget Mr. Ditteridge is a Superintendent, but Mrs. Ditteridge is just like you or me."

Linda hung up her coat. She was wearing a pale blue trouser suit that morning, with a little flowered apron tied round her waist. Her hair was still pink.

She started for the storeroom, stopped suddenly and turned back.

"What shall I do?" she asked. "There's seals on the door, and the vacuum and the polish and all my dusters are inside. What *shall* I do?... Oh, I know, wash the floor in here and the bathroom. I usually do that Thursdays but... No, the bucket's in there too. I'll have to tell Joe and see what he can do about it. I mean, we don't want the place going to wrack and ruin, do we? But there's not much I can do without my things, unless you could find me a rag, then I could do the brasses. And I could do the silver too, though it isn't due for it..." She began to plot her morning's work with a heavy frown on her face, as if murder, kidnapping and theft were of secondary importance to her inability to carry out her normal Monday programme.

Christine found an old pillowcase in the linen cupboard, ripped it into pieces and gave them to her. The brass polish was in the cupboard under the stairs. Linda armed herself with these and prepared to make an attack on the front doorbell, the knocker and letterbox.

"I was just remembering something yesterday," she said, as she put her coat on again against the cold that she would encounter on the doorstep. "Only a couple of years back we had a murder down our street. It got in the papers. Do you remember it? It was almost opposite us. I come home one afternoon after I'd been to the clinic with Maureen, and there was a crowd outside this house there. And I said, 'What is it?' And they said it was a murder. A young man murdered his father, they said, And one person said, 'He throttled him.' And another person said, 'He gassed him.' And another person said, 'No, he suffocated him, putting him in a cupboard.' And it turned out the truth was he'd throttled him, and then put him with his head in the gas oven, and then put him in a cupboard and turned the key on him."

"Good heavens, why did he do all that?" Christine asked.

"To make sure, I suppose."

"Yes, but I mean, why? What had he got against his father to do all that to him?"

"Well, it seems the young man came home and found his father assaulting his daughter, and he kind of went berserk." She paused and thought about it. "But it was just a murder, see? It wasn't a mystery. Not a *mystery*."

She went out, and a moment later was whistling quietly to herself as she polished the bell.

Christine was used to Linda's more gruesome stories by now, and the *sang-froid* with which she told them, though she knew that when Joe was on night duty and Linda had to sleep alone, she always took a sleeping pill, as Christine had the night before, to dispel her fear of the dark.

The morning passed very slowly. The telephone rang several times, but it was neither the police nor Lew, demanding ransom. Once it was Minna Maskell, asking how things were with them and suggesting that she should drop in for a little while, her intention being, Christine gathered, to cheer her up. Soon afterwards it was Vivien, also wanting to come to see her. She and Barry wanted to leave for

London soon, but the police had politely asked them to stay on for a little, and they were bored and restless. Christine told both Minna and Vivien about the disappearance of David and Frances. Minna, when she heard of it, exploded with excited sympathy, then became calmly practical.

"I think the *two* of them going off like that together is a good sign," she said. "What kidnapper is going to burden himself with two children, when one would do? I don't believe in this kidnapper idea at all, Christine. I'm sure the children simply got upset somehow, and decided to leave on their own, and as they can't have got far, or have much money, the police will soon find them. I know it's terrible for you, and I sympathise profoundly, but I'm sure all you have to do is keep your heads and wait."

Vivien's reaction was different. She was silent at first for so long that Christine thought that the connection had been broken. Then she heard her actually laugh.

"Do you know, I almost admire that horrible boy?" Vivien said. "He's got the art of making himself the centre of attention, hasn't he? It should carry him far in life. Don't worry about them, Christine. He's only done this to make you worry about him. Oh God, how well I know the type! My first husband was just the same. He'd have tantrums, make scenes, pack a suitcase and leave for ever, just to make sure I was thinking about him. Until I packed a suitcase and left for ever myself. In the end it was the only thing to do. And I've never once regretted it, although he was loaded with charm. As a matter of fact, your boy rather reminds me of him, all charm and complete selfishness. Well, Barry and I will be along in a little while. And don't worry too much. That type always turns up again, just when you'd begun to hope you were shot of them."

She rang off, leaving Christine more distracted than ever, because now she was angry with Vivien as well as worried about the children. How the friendship between herself and Vivien had survived all these years, she could not imagine. Vivien was hard-hearted, self-centred, unimaginative...The adjectives went on piling up, until, at about a quarter to twelve, she and Barry arrived.

Minna came a few minutes later, a brisk little cylinder of a woman in a suit of scarlet tweed, tripping forward on her neat little feet and kissing Christine warmly, then kissing Henry and also Marsha, and almost doing the same to Simon, but at the last moment drawing back and saying, "Let me see, I do know you, don't I? I know we've met before. No, don't tell me—I take pride in my memory for faces. But I keep meeting so many people..."

"My brother Simon," Henry said.

"Of *course!*" Minna said. "I've met you here, haven't I? I'd have remembered in another moment." She turned to Vivien. "I'm so glad to see you again, Mrs. Richmond. I've been wanting to tell you how immensely we enjoyed your talk on Saturday. May we hope that you'll come again some time? Mr. Richmond—so sad to meet in these circumstances, but perhaps we'll be able to tempt you back to Helsington with your wife on some other occasion. We have an Antiquarian Society, of which I happen to be the secretary. Might we hope that perhaps you'd come and address us on some subject of your own choosing at one of our meetings next year?"

Barry gave a friendly little bow, but as usual it was directed at Vivien, as if it were she who had asked the question, not Minna.

"Delighted," he said to his wife. "Most kind. Not that I'm an accomplished speaker, you understand. But anything I can do..."

Vivien made a little grimace at Christine, as if she wanted her to understand that once she and Barry were away from Helsington, nothing would ever persuade them to return. Christine could see her point of view, of course.

The doorbell rang.

Simon went out quickly to answer it, and in the moment after he was gone Christine felt a wild surge of hope that this was the police, returning David and Frances to them.

In fact it was the butcher, delivering the chops.

Presently the bell rang again, and this time it was the laundry man. Christine had forgotten that it was Monday, the day he called, and she had no parcel ready for him. The unimportant little incident helped to make her feel flustered and disorganised and that someone as incompetent as she was had never been fit to have care of children.

In the sitting room they had all settled down to drinks and she found herself wondering if she and Henry, when they were on their own, always drank as much as they had during the last day or two, or if this had been simply reaction to the exceptional circumstances. Then, of all times, she chose this time to start seriously worrying about the matter, getting annoyed with Henry, with herself, with their guests, for reaching out so automatically for this temporary solace. Under stress, she thought darkly, going to sit alone in the kitchen and brood on what to do about lunch, they all revealed themselves as potential alcoholics. And did that provide a good atmosphere for children? Did it give them any sense of stability, of security? Of course not. Henry and she had failed on all counts. They should never, never have let Ian and Ena entrust David and Frances to them.

Minna soon went home, but Vivien and Barry stayed on for lunch, a meal that had all come out of tins, and they were the only people who ate with any heartiness. Afterwards they said that they would go for a walk, and Barry suggested in his confiding way to Vivien that what Christine and Henry should do was have a good lie-down, and then come out to dinner with Barry and Vivien at the Crown.

She answered, "If those awful brats have come home, yes, of course, that would do them a lot of good. But can you imagine Henry and Christine tearing themselves away from the telephone if there's still no news?"

He admitted sadly, "No, I suppose not. But just to sit *waiting* . . . I do so immensely sympathise."

"Anyway, we'll call in later," Vivien said to Christine, "to hear if you've heard anything."

She and Barry left.

Henry suggested to Christine that she should follow Barry's advice and lie down. She rejected it abruptly. The afternoon dragged slowly and emptily by.

At about three o'clock the doorbell rang again and as before Simon went to answer it. Christine, in the sitting room, waited, tensely, listening. She heard men's voices, and realised that it was, in fact, the police. But there was something hushed and lugubrious about their tones which made her throat tighten with apprehension and set her heart pounding. Then she heard the front door close and there was silence. Then Simon's footsteps crossed the hall and he reappeared.

"Nothing," he said.

An hour passed. Then the telephone rang.

It was Christine who snatched it up, while Henry bounded upstairs to the extension in their bedroom.

The voice of Superintendent Ditteridge, sounding as moved as she had thought that it ever would only over something connected with his little bitch, Pippy, said, "We've got them!"

"David and Frances?"

"Yes, Mrs. Findon."

"Oh, thank God!"

"They're on their way back to you already. You've nothing to worry about."

"They're all right?"

"They're fine."

"They're really all right?"

"Couldn't be better."

"Where have they been?"

He hesitated, then said, "They've been with Lew Heacham in London."

"He *did* kidnap them, then!" she exploded. "I knew he wasn't much good, but I'd never have believed that of him."

"We-ell..." There was a pause. "It isn't as simple as that. If you don't mind, I think you'd better hear it from the children themselves. Meanwhile, you've nothing whatever to worry about. They're in a police car on their way back to Helsington, and they'll be with you in an hour or so."

Henry's voice came into the conversation then, expressing fervent thanks. Christine put the telephone down and at once began to cry. Marsha put an arm round her and began to cry too. Simon, looking for a moment as if he might be tempted to join in, muttered, "Oh, for God's sake!" and strode out to the kitchen, from which he presently

emerged with some very strong coffee. It was good medi-
cine. The next hour passed slowly, but by the time that the
doorbell rang again, they were all more or less in a state
of composure.

But it was not the police with David and Frances. It was
Vivien and Barry, back, not from a walk, but the cinema.

When they heard that the children had been found, Vivien
said, "Then you simply must come out to dinner with us.
All of you. It'll do you a lot of good. Yes, yes, yes"—as
Christine began to protest—"you simply must."

"Look, I'm not going to let those children out of my sight
again," Christine said. "I shall probably spend the night
sleeping on a mattress in the passage across their door."

"I'll really do that, if you like," Marsha said, "only, of
course, you wouldn't quite trust me. I let you down before,
didn't I?"

There was a short and suddenly surprisingly uncomfortable silence. It was as if it had taken this remark of Marsha's
to remind them that before the disappearance of the children,
there had been a murder in the house.

It was about six o'clock when the police car at last arrived
with David and Frances in it. David strolled into the house,
looking as unconcerned as he was able. Frances was carried
into it, sound asleep, by a sturdy young policewoman. Mr.
Ditteridge, following them, was accompanied by another
figure. Lew Heacham.

He walked into the sitting room, looking round it with
bright, defiant eyes. He was as neat as usual, his longish
hair was well brushed, but his face was pale and haggard
and his eyes circled with shadow, as if he had been going
short of sleep.

David stayed close to him. He was also white-faced from
fatigue, and there was something apprehensive in his eyes.
But Frances, whom the policewoman transferred to Henry's
arms, was rosy-cheeked and had a faint smile on her lips,
as if she were drowsily aware of the comfort of familiar
surroundings.

Christine opened her arms to David, but he hung back,
edging closer to Lew.

She turned on him. "Lew—how *could* you do such a thing?"

He threw up his head and echoed her in a mincing, mocking tone. "Lew! Lew! How could you do such a thing? That miserable Lew's let the side down again, hasn't he? We try so hard to be nice to him, but he's just no good at all. Look how he repays us! Accepts our hospitality, then runs out just when he might be useful to us as a suspect, and takes some of our precious snuffboxes with him. All the same, we understand poor Lew so well, and we're all so dreadfully sorry for him, we'll forgive him in the end. Oh yes, of course!"

"Superintendent," Christine said, raising her voice above Lew's, "where were they all? How did you find him and the children?"

"As a matter of fact, Mrs. Findon, he brought them to the police station himself," Mr. Ditteridge replied. "The police station in Camden Town."

"But why? I don't understand. What happened?"

"Perhaps it would be best if you let him explain it himself," Mr. Ditteridge said. "It wasn't exactly a case of kidnapping."

"Kidnapping!" Lew said shrilly. "Listen, if anyone was kidnapped, it was me! They came after me, found me, God knows how, and suggested that on what I could make, selling the snuffboxes, we could all go to South America. Well, if that wasn't kidnapping, it was blackmail, wasn't it? And what was I to do. I'd nowhere to take them and even if I had, I could only see trouble ahead, lots of trouble. So I tried to make them see sense and leave me in peace and go home on the train. But have you ever tried to make this boy David do something he didn't want to? So I didn't let on to them where I was really taking them, and then I just popped into the police station with them."

David slid a hand into Lew's. "We weren't really blackmailing you, Lew," he said in a tone of apology. "We just came because we were fond of you, and we didn't think anyone was being fair to you, any more than to me, saying I'd stolen those shoes."

"A nice way you've got of showing your affection, then," Lew said, "making me turn myself in when I could have got clean away."

"It doesn't sound as if you'd have got clean away very easily," Henry said, "if the children found you so quickly. How *did* they find you?"

"He told us where to find him," David said.

"Told you? Never!" Lew exclaimed. "It was magic, that's what it was. Telepathy. Extrasensory-whatsit. It's got me scared stiff. The kid's uncanny. I don't think I've ever been as frightened in my life as I was when the two of them walked into the Three Dragons, where I'd gone to talk to a friend about the snuffboxes, and asked for me. Old Harry behind the bar was frightened too—kids like them walking into his pub in broad daylight, as if that was the most normal thing in the world. He bellowed at them to get out quick. He asked them if they didn't know better than to try going into pubs at their age, getting him into trouble. And I thought of dodging out the back way, but then they saw me and threw their arms round me as if they were ready to choke me to death. And then, believe it or not, they started saying they were hungry and that they hadn't any money. So what could I do but take them to a café and spend my own cash on them. Eat! Sausages, beans, chips, chocolate éclairs, Cokes—it nearly cleared me out. And then they wouldn't go home even if I paid their fares for them!"

David's face was looking inclined to crumple tearfully, though he was struggling to resist it.

Henry returned to his question. "But how did you know you'd find Lew at the Three Dragons, David?"

"He told us, he told us!" David answered with one of his brief flares of temper. "That day while he was helping Frances do the jigsaw puzzle and I was writing, and I wished Lew would be quiet so I could concentrate properly, but he kept talking, telling us stories and so on, and Frances asked him where he lived and he said he lived here and there-but you could generally find him in the palace of the Three Dragons. And then he laughed a lot, as if he'd said something clever, and I knew of course it wasn't true, you wouldn't find him in any palace. But I thought, Mummy and Daddy like a pub called the Seven Mermaids. So I thought, it's a pub, and when we got to London we looked in the telephone book, and there it was, the Three Dragons, in Camden Town. So we asked the way and took a bus, and that's all there was to it. And we thought he'd be glad to see us. We thought with everyone else being against us, like they were against him, he'd stick by us."

"All there was to it," Mr. Ditteridge murmured. "It's a bit premature, perhaps, but if ever you should be looking for a job, David . . ."

Lew was looking uncomfortable. "Well, David, I did really stick by you," he said, "and didn't mean to let you down. What I did—I thought it was the best for you."

"And it was best for yourself too, probably," Simon said with a sardonic smile. "Since you've demonstrated so clearly you've a heart of gold, I don't see anyone worrying much about the snuffboxes."

"Of course not," Henry said. "Superintendent, if Lew Heacham wasn't responsible for the disappearance of the children, we wouldn't want to press charges against him about the snuffboxes. I'm almost inclined to say, let him keep them, if he wants them so badly. He is, after all, almost a member of the family—"

"Listen to him!" Lew broke in. "Bloody understanding old Henry—so bloody, bloody understanding! But I don't belong to your family, and I don't want to, Henry. I don't want to belong anywhere. I belong to myself."

"It isn't just a question of snuffboxes, Mr. Findon," Mr. Ditteridge said, ignoring Lew. "Nor even of the children either. There's the question of murder."

There was a sudden silence in the room.

It made Christine realise what a noise they had all just been making with their voices raised and constantly interrupting one another. But the complete silence lasted only for an instant. Then Simon moved closer to Marsha and put an arm round her shoulders, and she leant against him, as if she found that a comfort. Barry Richmond, who had been staring at Lew, turned his head to gaze again at Vivien, and she moved a step nearer to him. Henry rubbed his forehead with his knuckles.

Christine was the one who spoke, "And that's why you brought Lew back here, Superintendent? It wasn't because of the children, or the snuffboxes."

"He came of his own free will," Mr. Ditteridge said, "to help us with our inquiries."

"So why don't you get on, doing some inquiring?" Lew said, trying to keep up his aggressive tone, yet sounding all at once subdued and forlorn. "She wasn't much to me, but she was my mother. I'll help if I can."

"Then tell us what you meant when you said that that boy had told you everything that you wanted to know," Mr. Ditteridge said.

"I didn't mean anything," Lew said.

"You must have."

"I didn't."

"What had the boy told you?"

"Not a thing."

"Not a thing," David echoed him. "I was just fooling about. I told you so."

"Yet you shouted out that he'd told you everything you wanted to know," Mr. Ditteridge said to Lew, "then you rushed up to your room, and that afternoon you took off for London, with the snuffboxes in your pocket."

"All right, so I did."

"You aren't going to tell us anything more about it?"

"There's nothing more to tell."

Mr. Ditteridge looked at Henry. "You were there when it happened, weren't you, Mr. Findon?"

Henry nodded.

Mr. Ditteridge looked round the room. "You were all there except Mr. Richmond."

"You were there yourself," Simon said.

"That's right," Mr. Ditteridge agreed. "So I'm going to tell you how I remember it, and I'd like you to stop me if any of you thinks I'm wrong. To begin with, then, the boy came out of the study. He was limping, because he'd got on one high-heeled shoe. It was one of Mrs. Richmond's collection, a green shoe with a silver buckle and a red heel. He must have taken it from her suitcase a few minutes before."

"As he took my other shoes," Vivien said. "In my opinion the boy's not merely a thief, he's abnormal. He's got a thing about shoes."

Mr. Ditteridge took no notice of her. "He was also carrying a cane with an ivory handle. It was the cane Mrs. Richmond used the night before when she was pretending she'd a sprained ankle. It was normally kept in the storeroom, in a corner behind the trunk in which Mrs. Heacham's body was found. Mr. Findon got it for Mrs. Richmond shortly before you all set off for the dinner. In doing it he appears to have got some blood on to his cuff."

"I don't understand," Vivien said as he paused briefly. "Do you mean Mrs. Heacham was already dead then?"

Mr. Ditteridge again took no notice of her. "The boy was also carrying a snuffbox," he said. "It was a gold one, with a monogram in rubies on the lid."

"And he pretended to take snuff," Christine said, "and he said 'Egad! Odd's fish! By my hallidom!'"

"And Lew Heacham said that the boy had told him everything that he wanted to know and ran upstairs," Mr. Ditteridge went on.

"I don't understand," Vivien repeated. "Why won't you tell us what you meant, Lew?"

He only glowered at her.

Mr. Ditteridge replied, "I think he won't talk, Mrs. Richmond, because he still hopes to be paid for what he knows. That's your line, isn't it, Heacham, in spite of your heart of gold. Money for silence."

"But what does he know?" Christine asked.

"Think of what he actually saw," Mr. Ditteridge said. There had been a change in his voice and his face. At that moment Christine could not have imagined him fondling and crooning over Pippy. He looked as if he were hard right through. "He saw a shoe with a red heel. He saw a gold snuffbox with red letters on the lid. Red on a shoe. Red on gold. Blood on a golden sandal—that's what he saw—Mrs. Richmond, you got blood on your evening sandal, didn't you, when your husband killed Mrs. Heacham in the storeroom?"

Vivien gave a start. Her face went blank with amazement.

Then her gaze became piercing, as if she were really seeing him for the first time.

"Has everyone gone mad?" she asked.

Mr. Ditteridge shook his head and in a flat voice uttered the formal words of the official warning.

"But you're mad, mad!" she cried. "Why should Barry kill Mrs. Heacham? What should either of us have been doing in the storeroom?"

"Your motive?" Mr. Ditteridge said. "It isn't necessary to prove motive, you know. But I should think Mr. Richmond wanted that collection of snuffboxes. He's keen about things like that. He's curator of the Blanchland Museum, only the things he looks after there don't belong to him, and perhaps he wanted to have something of his own for once. And these were going to be so easy to get hold of, with you in the house, Mrs. Richmond, to let him in, and everyone else going out. That's what you thought, anyway. You didn't know how many people there'd be in the house, or that Mrs. Heacham would be restless and worried and prowling around."

"It's crazy, every word of it!" Vivien exclaimed, but there was desperation in her voice. "You talked about blood on my sandal. What did you mean?"

"Oh, it was the sandal that trapped you," he said, "because you had to get rid of it quickly, yet you had to wear evening dress, and you'd brought only one pair of evening shoes with you. So to cover up the fact that it was just the gold shoe that was missing, you got all your left shoes and gave them to your husband to get rid of, planning to make it look as if the boy had played a malicious trick on you by stealing them. And as there happened to be the remains of a bonfire burning in the garden, your husband dumped the shoes on it, pushing the sandal well down into the middle of the fire, where it would be destroyed... The tragedy is, you'd never meant to commit murder, had you? Mr. Findon's right, it was meant to be quite a small crime, as crimes go. If only Mrs. Heacham hadn't come down to talk to her son, and heard something in the storeroom and looked in and found you, no one would have died. But of course she recognised Mr. Richmond, who wasn't supposed to be there, and who couldn't think quickly enough to explain how he happened to be hiding in the storeroom. All he could think of was using a hammer. And after that you had to hide the body, and destroy the bloodstained sandal and he had to get clear. So you decided to give up the idea of stealing the collection. Your little crime had turned into a very big one. A completely pointless one too, with nothing gained by anybody. I'm told you gave a good talk that evening, Mrs. Richmond. I'm told it was a success. That's something I can almost admire."

Vivien was standing very straight. There was a hectic flush on her cheekbones, and her eyes were unnaturally bright.

"You've no proof—" she began, but Barry reached out, caught hold of her hand and pressed it so hard that she winced. As usual he spoke to her, apparently ignoring the existence of Mr. Ditteridge and everyone else in the room. He and Vivien might have been alone together.

"No proof at all, of course. That goes without saying. So I should say nothing, my dear. Nothing at all."

# 10

But, as Mr. Ditteridge said to them later, it is surprising what you can find in the way of proof when you know where to look.

During the next few days the police found a spot of blood on the under side of the hem of the evening dress that Vivien had worn to the dinner of the Costume Society. The blood group was the same as Mrs. Heacham's. They also found dust on a suit of Barry's which, in its curious composition, matched that of the dust in the storeroom. They found some traces of ashes which matched those of the bonfire in the ridges of the rubber soles of a pair of Barry's shoes.

Then Vivien broke down and began confessing everything.

At first, when Christine heard of it, this surprised her. She had thought that Vivien was of a much tougher fibre than Barry. But later, when it came to the trial, Christine came to the conclusion that Vivien had broken down only after having given some careful thought to the advantages of doing so. For by presenting herself as someone who was helplessly under the influence of her husband, she was given a sentence of only five years, while Barry got life. By cooperating with the police, even if she was not able to give evidence against her husband, Vivien got off lightly.

Then there was the fact, which Barry never disputed, that Vivien had not actually held the hammer that had killed

Mrs. Heacham. Indeed, by the time her defence had had
its say, the court had been given a picture of her desperately
trying to control her husband and save Mrs. Heacham's life.
And why should this not have been the truth? Vivien had
always been a clear-thinking, hard-headed woman, and she
would have seen the utter folly of that killing when her
frightened husband had not. All that they had had to lose,
after all, if Barry had been discovered skulking in the house,
was the Findons' friendship. And even that might have
survived. The Findons might have been puzzled at his odd
behaviour, but probably would have accepted it as a rather
touching display of his need for Vivien. So perhaps Vivien
truly had tried to stop him doing murder. Christine found
it comforting, for old times' sake, to think so.

After the police took the Richmonds away from the house
that day, the Findons did not see them again until the trial,
when Henry and Christine had to be witnesses. By then they
knew more or less what had happened in their house on the
night of the Costume Society's Annual Dinner. They had
remembered some odds and ends too, which seemed too
insignificant to tell the police, but which added to their own
picture of the events of that evening. For instance, Vivien's
tiredness, much advertised by her, when she arrived in
Helsington. She had insisted on resting, on having an hour
to herself. During that time Barry, of course, had been
waiting outside in the darkness, until Vivien had seen that
the coast was clear and had slipped down to let him in by
the back door. There was the fact, too, that when she had
first met Marsha, Vivien had become very thoughtful. She
had not known before of the presence of Marsha or Lew
in the house, and must have wondered when she found them
there if the whole plan had better not be abandoned. But
when it came to the point, they had not caused her any
difficulties. It was Mrs. Heacham who had strayed accidentally into the heart of the plot and been dealt with.

Soon after the police had taken the Richmonds away, the
Findons' telephone had started ringing again and again with
messages of sympathy about the missing children, for Minna
Maskell had been at work on her own telephone, and because it is almost impossible not to answer that shrill, in-

trusive sound, however much you may want not to, either Christine or Henry had had to collect their wits and make noises of some kind back into the mouthpiece. After a little, Simon had taken this job on himself. He had said firmly to each caller that Henry and Christine were engaged and could not be disturbed, but would of course be told of the kind inquiry. He had also been very adroit in giving out a minimum of information without discourtesy. Marsha had shown a tendency to linger near him when he was doing this, as if ready to prompt him if his imagination should run dry, and once, when he had put the telephone down, he had got up, taken her in his arms and kissed her long and hard. Christine did not know what happened after that, because she had gone away and left them.

She and Henry had put the children to bed, and from the calm of Henry's tone, as they did so, no one could have guessed what horrors he and Christine had been through on the children's account that day. She had not joined in. She had not trusted herself to keep her emotions out of her voice. She might have started crying in the middle, or got angry, or exploded with joyful relief, and altogether given the pair an exaggerated idea of their importance. She had been sure that Henry was right to play the incident down from the beginning, but to have done this would have been beyond her just then.

The children had slept most of the next day, curled up in chairs in the sitting room, then they had gone early to bed, worn out by their adventure. By agreement, Henry and Christine had hardly questioned them about it. There was to be no dramatization of the incident. Henry's unconcern had remained marvellously convincing, and Christine's, though she had felt that it would not have deceived an imbecile, had been a careful imitation of his. They had all begun to calm down.

Next morning Simon had gone back to London. Henry had returned to his teaching. Marsha had gone to some lectures at her Domestic Science college. David had started writing a new novel.

That evening Simon had rung up from London. He had spoken briefly to Henry, but it had really been Marsha whom

he had wanted, and from that evening on, telephone calls
from Simon had become a frequent occurrence. When Marsha reappeared after taking them, she had generally had a
glow in her cheeks and a radiance about her that made her
breathtaking. She knitted away hard at the blue and green
sweater that she was making for Christine, and would make
sudden gestures of excited affection to her, to Henry and
the children. She was the kind of girl who, when she falls
in love, falls a little in love with everyone and everything,
and needs to show it.

Christine got back into the way of doing the shopping
and cooking. It was more difficult than she had expected.
She seemed to have forgotten everything that she had ever
known about it. But also, mysteriously, she seemed to have
far more time than she had had when she had had nothing
to do, so when Joe Deeping had painted the storeroom, she
had got rid of most of the junk in it, and turned it into a
workroom, where she could write, paint, dressmake, and
try her hand at some modelling in clay, in which she had
started taking some evening classes.

But that all came about later, naturally. Cooking was the
only job that she had had to tackle immediately. One day
she decided to be a little bit venturesome and made a *mous-
saka*, and in her own opinion it was a success and both she
and Henry were eating it with enjoyment when they noticed
that the children were both looking with loathing at what
was on their plates. Christine was annoyed with herself
then. She ought to have known that this was just the kind
of dish which no child who had not been brought up to such
things would dream of touching. The extreme conservatism
of children in matters of food had been made very clear to
her within a few days of the arrival of David and Frances
in Helsington. But hell hath no fury like a woman whose
cooking has been scorned, so she snapped at them more
irritably than usual, "What's the matter?"

In answer, Frances let her knife and fork clatter on her
plate and gave a loud wail. Tears begun to pour down her
face.

"I want Mrs. Heacham!" she cried. "I *loved* Mrs. Heacham! She made lovely dumplings for us!"

Bouncing off her chair, she fled from the room.

So Mrs. Heacham had at least one generous epitaph. She had not lived her arid life entirely in vain.

David messed the mince and *aubergines* about on his plate and muttered, "She's silly."

"If you don't want to eat that, leave it!" Christine said.

"I'd like some pork pie," he said.

"There isn't any pork pie," she answered. "If you don't want that, you can go hungry."

He gave her a startled look, never having heard that tone from her before.

"Are you angry?" he asked mildly. "I thought you didn't get angry." Then all at once he started to cry too. "If you say I'm a thief and a liar and a murderer, I shall run away again!" he shouted at her. "I won't stay anywhere they call me a thief and liar and a murderer!"

Christine and Henry exchanged quick looks, then Henry said quietly, "We know you aren't a thief and a liar, David. That was all a mistake, for which everyone was very sorry. And no one ever called you a murderer."

"But I *am* one!" David cried.

"Are you really?" Henry said.

"Yes, it's all my fault," David said through his sobs. "I told Mrs. Heacham about the Red Indians in the storeroom, and I said one day they'd jump out at her and scalp her. Of course it was just a joke. I only said it to frighten her. I didn't believe it. And then—then it happened!"

"So when you went looking for Lew, you were really running away from the Red Indians, were you?" Henry said.

"Well, partly," David said. "I was frightened."

"Do you know, Red Indians are about the only people I never suspected of killing Mrs. Heacham," Henry said. "I don't think you need worry about them any more."

David was looking exceedingly young. Sometimes he could look so grown-up, so mature, but just then he was looking about six years old.

"Of course, I know I was just pretending, there aren't really any Red Indians in there, but I got frightened."

"You knew you'd invented them, yet you got frightened of them?" Henry said.

David nodded wretchedly.

"Well, there's nothing for frightening one out of one's wits like one's own mind," Henry said gravely. "Unluckily, it's the one thing one can't run away from."

Christine cleared the plates away and produced a treacle tart. Then she went to find Frances, to see if she would consent to come and eat and be comforted.

They had the children with them until nearly Christmas, when their parents came home from America. Only a few days after they had gone, Simon and Marsha got married. Christine and Henry were witnesses at their wedding and they all had lunch together afterwards at the Europa in Charlotte Street, then Simon and Marsha left for Italy and Henry and Christine went back to a strangely quiet house in Helsington.

Lew vanished after the trial as abruptly as he had appeared. Henry and Christine did not try to find him.

But the house seemed absurdly large for just two people, and eerily quiet.

It took Christine longer than she had expected to begin to get used to that continuing quiet.

## ABOUT THE AUTHOR

E. X. FERRARS lives in Scotland with her husband who is a professor at the University of Edinburgh. She is the author of many crime novels, including *The Pretty Pink Shroud*, *Blood Flies Upwards*, *The Cup and the Lip*, and *Drowned Rat*. When not concocting mysteries of her own, she enjoys traveling, or the mysteries of cooking and gardening—and reading other writers' mysteries.

"The most important horror collection of the year."
—*Locus*

# DARK FORCES

## Edited by Kirby McCauley

(14801-x)          $3.50

**Including a complete new short novel by Stephen King**

This new volume of 23 chillers contains new works by a star-studded roster of authors. You'll find spine-tingling tales from Davis Grubb, Ray Bradbury, Edward Gorey, Robert Aickman, Joe Haldeman, Dennis Etchison, Karl Edward Wagner, Lisa Tuttle, Ramsey Campbell, T.E.D. Klein, and many other masters of horror.

Get ready for terror as you encounter slug-like creatures who inhabit New York City's sewers, zombies who become all-night store clerks in California, a young boy who is kidnapped in his very own bed, and a multitude of horrifying beings and events.

*A triumphant novel of passion, danger and romance from bestselling novelists*

# PATRICIA MATTHEWS
## and
# CLAYTON MATTHEWS

# MIDNIGHT WHISPERS

Patricia Matthews is one of America's bestselling romantic storytellers. Now, for the first time, she has teamed up with her husband, popular novelist Clayton Matthews, to create a stunning contemporary tale.

*MIDNIGHT WHISPERS* is the story of April Morgan, a beautiful young heiress whose witness of a shocking event has erased her memory. From Cape Cod's untamed coast to the jagged cliffs of Ireland, from the lake country of Switzerland to fast-paced, trendy London, April searches for her hidden past and finds romance in the arms of a sophisticated Irish actor and a passionate young clothes designer. But wherever she goes, she is haunted by a mysterious voice on the phone— "Mr. Midnight," a total stranger with the power to manipulate April's every move—for good or for evil.

*Read MIDNIGHT WHISPERS, available October 15, wherever Bantam Books are sold.*

# Masters
## *of*
# Mystery

With these new mystery titles, Bantam takes you to the scene of the crime. These masters of mystery follow in the tradition of the great British and American crime writers. Maud Silver, Chief Inspector Damiot, and Inspector Rhys—you'll meet these talented sleuths as they get to the bottom of even the most baffling crimes.